Barely aware of what he was doing, he deliberately turned her to face him, bent his head, and caught her mouth under his.

He didn't know how long he moved over her lips, but he did know he never wanted to stop. She was sweet beyond belief, and soft. And female. So female he ached all over.

"Don't you ever, *ever* do that again!" she shouted, pulling away.

He could see her body shaking; the ruffles down the front of her shirtwaist trembled. He stared at her. Her eyes blazed into his and without thinking he reached for her arm.

"St_ _away," she warned. "Just stay away f_ _me."

_he—? He stepped back but couldn't _ _ooking at her. He'd never misjudged a _ _ _n this badly since he was a green boy of _ _ _en.

Author Note

Women in the Old West struggled to be treated as equals, to own property in their own names and to exercise their right to vote—things we take for granted in today's America.

This story reminds us that such rights had to be fought for.

HER SHERIFF BODYGUARD

Lynna Banning

MILLS &
BOON

Published in Great Britain 2016
by Mills & Boon, an imprint of HarperCollins*Publishers*
1 London Bridge Street, London, SE1 9GF

© 2016 The Woolston Family Trust

ISBN: 978-0-263-91719-2

Our policy is to use papers that are natural, renewable and
recyclable products and made from wood grown in sustainable
forests. The logging and manufacturing processes conform to the
legal environmental regulations of the country of origin.

Printed and bound in Spain
by CPI, Barcelona

Lynna Banning combines her lifelong love of history and literature in a satisfying career as a writer. Born in Oregon, she graduated from Scripps College and embarked on a career as an editor and technical writer, and later as a high school English teacher. She enjoys hearing from her readers. You may write to her directly at PO Box 324, Felton, CA 95018, USA, email her at carowoolston@att.net or visit Lynna's website at lynnabanning.net.

In memory of my mother, Mary Banning Yarnes,
and my grandmother, Leora Boessen Banning,
both of whom quietly lived lives that
enhanced the inherent rights of women.

Prologue

I, Fernanda Elena Maria Sobrano, am tell you this thing from my heart, how I find this man, Hawk Rivera, and ask for his help. My lady she not know what I do, but you will understand when I tell what happen.

Chapter One

"Sheriff, you can't miss this."

Hawk Rivera tilted his head so he could see the pudgy overeager face of the mayor from beneath the broad brim of his well-worn gray Stetson. "Like hell I can't."

"But everybody in town'll be there!"

Hawk winced. All the more reason he should stay away. It wasn't that he didn't like the townspeople of Smoke River, just that he didn't like them in bunches. "Mingling," his mother had called it. He hated mingling. Made the back of his neck crawl like two dozen spiders had been dropped down his shirt collar. Mayor O'Grady cleared his throat. "She came in on the afternoon train. Fine-looking woman."

Hawk shifted his boots to a new spot on his paper-littered desk. "Save your breath, Harve. Not interested."

"Looks kinda feisty, too."

"Still not interested."

Harvey O'Grady smacked his now-empty whiskey glass down on top of a Wanted poster. "Not interested in a pretty woman? Somethin' wrong with you, Sheriff."

Hawk snorted. "Nuthin' wrong with me another shot of whiskey and a little peace and quiet can't fix. Leave me alone, Harve." He tipped his chair farther back toward the dirty wall of the jail. "Leave the whiskey."

"Aw, hell. A little excitement'd do ya good. Sure as God made little green leprechauns, yer gettin' morose as a randy coyote."

"Drop it, Harve." Pointedly he looked at the door. "See you tomorrow."

His office door slammed and Hawk reached for his whiskey, drained the glass, then refilled it from the flask the mayor had left. Night was too damn pretty to spoil it with politics.

Down the street somewhere he heard what sounded like chanting. "Oregon women better take note, Wyoming women have got the vote!"

He snorted. Bad poem. Bad idea. If Oregon women were smart they'd leave the thinking to their menfolk and tend to the business of making love and babies. Like they did in Texas.

But that's why you left, isn't it? Love and a baby?

He gritted his teeth so hard his jaw cracked. He grabbed for his whiskey and shut his eyes.

Caroline MacFarlane leaned out the second floor window of her hotel room and pointed. "Just look, Fernanda. The ladies have made signboards!"

Below her in the street a dozen women marched holding up hand-lettered placards.

LADIES UNITE.
WOMEN ARE PEOPLE TOO.
VOTES FOR WOMEN!

With their free hands, the ladies gripped their straw bonnets, which the hot afternoon breeze threatened to dislodge. Caroline's eyes filled with tears.

"Oh, Mama would have been so proud."

Fernanda shifted her bulk beside her. "Your mama, *mi corazón*, work too hard."

True. Her mother had never minded the dust, or the heat, or the rough manners of little towns like this one, out in the middle of nowhere. Evangeline MacFarlane had lived for The Cause. Caroline was doing her best to follow in her sainted mother's footsteps.

Fernanda touched her arm. "You must eat something before people come."

"Afterward," Caroline breathed. "I am far too excited to eat just now."

"Humph," Fernanda sniffed. "Soon you look like scrawny chicken. Now you put on speaking dress."

Reluctantly Caroline let her companion draw her away from the window, lace her up in the whalebone corset that made it hard to breathe between sentences and smooth out the sleeves on her severely cut dark blue bombazine. She must look every inch a lady tonight; winning over an audience of ranchers and townspeople and their wives must be handled with decorum as well as rousing words.

With a final tug at her starched petticoats she donned her favorite speech-making hat, a bonnet with an iridescent green-and-blue pheasant feather drooping stylishly over one eye. She flashed Fernanda a smile and turned toward the door.

"Let us go forth and conquer!"

Even from inside his office, Hawk could hear the noise rumbling from the town hall behind the barbershop. A twinge of unease crawled up the back of his neck. He hadn't heard such a commotion since the lynching the new judge, Jericho Silver, had narrowly averted. That, he recalled grimly, had ended up in a near riot.

He was glad Jericho had been elected district judge. That had meant Smoke River had needed a new sheriff. And he'd sure as hell needed to get out of Texas.

He liked Smoke River. The town was flanked by mountains that shaded into purple in the distance, golden wheat fields, and endless grassy expanses where mottled brown cows grazed. Like Butte City, only smaller. Tree-lined streets. Nice houses. Even the main street looked well-kept.

His deputy cracked open the door and peered across the street. "They're gettin' kinda riled up, Sheriff."

"Let 'em. Words never hurt anybody."

"I dunno," Sandy said. He pulled his blond head back inside the jail and shut the door. "All the men are lined up on one side and the women are on the other. Haven't stopped yellin' at each other for the last half hour."

Hawk thunked his boots onto the dirty plank floor. "All right, I'll go have a look. You stay here and keep a cell open in case some damn fool troublemaker needs cooling off."

He straightened his hat, checked his Colt and swung out the door onto the board sidewalk. Raucous catcalls drifted from across the street and he quickened his pace.

Inside the stifling hall overwrought women waved placards while the men taunted. Hawk frowned. All this uproar over a simple little speech? For a moment he considered tramping back across to the jail and letting them fight it out, but then he caught sight of a trim female figure in a dark blue dress and an interesting-looking hat and he changed his mind.

She had dark hair pulled into a neat-looking twist at the nape of her neck. He couldn't see her eyes, but the tilt of her chin looked determined enough to stop a cattle stampede. She ploughed her way up the aisle between the two warring factions like an implacable ship on choppy seas and took her place behind the improvised lectern, two stacked apple crates at the far end of the room.

She stood there for a good four minutes while the ladies yelled and carried on and the men shouted. At last she raised both arms and quiet descended.

The sudden silence felt odd. Tension boiled in the room, and when the woman dropped her arms and opened her lips, Hawk's instincts signaled trouble.

"Ladies," she began. "And gentlemen." She put subtle emphasis on the word. "We are about to change history."

The women cheered. The glowering men sat with their arms clamped across their bellies.

"We must take our future into our own hands. We must…"

Something about her low, melodious voice curled around his gut like smoke on a hot summer night. The women hung on every word, their faces rapt, while the men roared their disapproval and heckled when she stopped to draw breath.

"Go back to Boston, girlie!"

"Our women don't want the vote."

"Oh, yes we do!" a woman screeched. She leaped to her feet and pounded the tip of her parasol on the wooden floor.

"Siddown and shut up," a male voice yelled.

To her credit the speaker waited for the tumult to die down before continuing. But she did continue. Hawk rolled his eyes at the inflammatory stuff she was saying, but he had to admit she had courage. A smart person would edge on out the back door.

"Gentlemen," she called, after a particularly ugly outburst of catcalls. "Gentlemen, let me ask you a question."

"Save it, honey!" someone yelled from the back of the room.

"No, I will not 'save it,' sir. Hear me out. Did you know that here in Oregon a married woman cannot—?"

"Sure we know all about that, lady. Keeps our women right where we want 'em."

"And where is that, sir?"

"Underneath a man with her legs spread, where else?"

The men guffawed while screams of outrage erupted from the women, and the shouting match resumed.

Hawk heaved a tired sigh. Enough was enough. He didn't favor women's right to vote, but he did support law and order. He strode forward down the aisle separating the warring parties, counting on his presence and the revolver he wore on his hip to calm things down. Deliberately he moved toward the woman behind the apple crates and the noise of the crowd dropped.

He drew close enough to her to note that she had very, very rosy lips, and then suddenly a gun went off somewhere behind him. A bullet thunked into one of the crates.

Hawk dove forward and threw himself on top of her, toppling her to the floor under him. A second shot whined past his head.

Pandemonium erupted. Women screamed, men yelled and somewhere outside a dog began to bark.

"Don't move," he ordered the woman pinned beneath him. "Lie still."

Her body twitched, but she said nothing.

He heard the dog yelp and go quiet. Gradually the noise inside the meeting hall faded to an uneasy buzz, and he rolled off her and onto his feet, revolver drawn.

A sea of stunned faces stared back at him.

"She okay?" a male voice asked.

"I—I am quite well, thank you," the woman

spoke at his back. He heard a rustle of petticoats and he guessed she was getting to her feet. He kept his weapon trained on the crowd, but no one moved or spoke.

He holstered his sidearm. "Meeting's over, folks. Go on home unless you want to spend the night in jail."

The hall emptied like a beer keg on Saturday night and Hawk turned to the woman. Damn suffragettes. Stirred up trouble everywhere they went.

Her fancy hat was mashed flat and her hair was straggling out of her bun. A plump Mexican woman darted from the crowd and began brushing the dust off the now-rumpled dark blue dress.

"Stop, Fernanda," the woman urged, batting at her hands. "We will take care of this later."

"I'll see you to your hotel, ma'am."

She trained the bluest eyes he'd ever seen on him and did not smile. "Thank you, Sheriff, but that will not be necessary. I am perfectly capable of walking."

"Might be capable all right, but unless you're carrying a pistol in your skirt pocket, you're not armed. Come on."

He grasped her elbow. She wrenched free, but he grabbed her arm again and moved her toward the entrance. The Mexican woman followed them out the door and down the street to the hotel.

"What's her room number, Ed?" he growled as he marched her past the front desk.

The balding desk clerk gulped. "Two-ten. Top of the—"

"Right." He snagged the key from the rack, guided both women up the stairs, and shooed them into the safety of their room. "Throw the bolt," he ordered.

Then he tipped his hat and stalked back down the staircase. Before he returned to the jail he scouted the town from the livery stable at one end to the church at the other, nosed around the saloon and spent the better part of an hour studying fresh hoofprints in the road.

Nothing. Whoever had fired those shots was long gone.

Or the bastard was still in town. It was then he began to taste fear in the back of his throat. Someone was gunning for her.

Chapter Two

Before Hawk could pour himself another shot of whiskey, the jail door banged open and the Mexican woman barreled into his office. Her long braid of black hair was sliced with silver and her large dark eyes snapped with impatience.

"Ah, *señor*, I am glad to have find you."

Hawk removed his boots from his desk, planted them on the floor and stood up. "You found me, all right, *señora*. Question is why?" He motioned for her to take the straight-back chair beside his desk.

"You are *Señor* Anderson Rivera, are you not? The one they call Hawk?"

"Yeah, I'm sometimes called that. Who are you?"

"I am Fernanda Elena Maria Sobrano. From Tejas. I knew your mother."

Hawk narrowed his eyes. "What part of Texas?"

"Butte City. Your mother was Marguerite Anderson, no? You look much like her, *señor*. Your eyes. Green, like hers."

Hawk could count on the fingers of one hand the times he'd thought of his mother in the past twelve years. He topped up his drink, then lifted the bottle toward the woman. "Whiskey?"

At her nod, he pulled a clean shot glass from his desk drawer and filled it.

"Salud!" She took a small sip. Hawk lifted his own glass and downed a hefty gulp.

"Salud. Señora Sobrano, what—?"

"We need your help, Miss MacFarlane and I." She sipped again.

"What for?"

"Is dangerous, this speaking. You see what happen tonight, no?"

"I saw it. I stopped it. What more do you want?"

Señora Sobrano tapped one finger against her glass. "Someone shoot at her last week, also, in the city of Salt Lake. But she do not give up, Señor Hawk. Tomorrow after tomorrow, Miss Caroline, she make speech in Gillette Springs."

"Not my problem, *señora*. They've got a sheriff up there, name of Davis. Good man."

"Is not a sheriff we need, I think. I think this someone follows us to kill Miss Caroline."

"You mean someone is stalking her? Because she's making speeches?"

"Si."

"Then maybe she should stop making speeches."

The woman gave him a long, considering look. "Miss Caroline, she will not stop. She cannot."

"Then she's not as smart as she looks."

"Is not a matter of smart, *Señor* Hawk. Is a matter of pride. Her mother makes speeches before her, but she die from the lungs in Tejas.

In Butte City. Miss Caroline say is her duty to continue."

"Stubborn, too," Hawk observed drily.

"*Sí*. But even when someone shoots at her, she does not give up. So now I ask you…"

"No."

She didn't even blink. "I know of you, *señor*. In Tejas you were a Ranger. I know such a man seeks to protect."

"The answer is still No."

She went on as if he hadn't spoken. "I ask you to protect Miss Caroline."

"She needs a bodyguard, *señora*. I'm a sheriff now, not a Ranger. I don't 'protect' anymore."

"Your mother would not believe. Your mother would be proud."

Hawk sat back and studied the woman across from him. Yeah, he'd have done almost anything to make his mother proud. But not this. This cut too close to the bone.

"Miss Caroline know you're here?"

"Oh, no, *señor*. She would not like."

"Then why—"

"Because I promise Miss Caroline's mother to keep her safe." Her keen black eyes held his. "This I cannot do alone. But you can do. Your *madre* would want you to do this."

Hawk paused, then tossed back the rest of his whiskey. "Sandy," he yelled.

"Yeah?" his deputy called from the jail cells.

"I'm riding out tomorrow morning."

Sandy ambled into his office. "Where ya goin', Sheriff?"

"Gillette Springs. Keep the peace here till I get back." He gulped down the last of his whiskey and rose.

"Now, *Señora* Sobrano, let's go on over to the hotel and make a plan."

"Are you out of your mind, Sheriff?" Caroline clutched her blue silk robe about her and shot Fernanda a look of fury.

"Nope, just cautious."

She advanced on him and poked her forefinger into his chest. "Well, let me tell you something, Sheriff. Caution is not going to win the vote for women."

"Neither is getting yourself killed, Miss MacFarlane. Whoever shot at you tonight is probably still in the vicinity."

"So?"

"So I don't figure he's going to give up."

"I have traveled all over the West, from Colorado to Utah to Texas and now to Oregon. Yes, there are those who try to stop me, but I will not give up."

"You don't have to give up. You just have to be sensible." He tossed the package he'd brought from the mercantile onto the bed. Fernanda pounced on it.

Caroline sent her a quelling look, but she was too absorbed in undoing the wrapping to notice. "What does 'sensible' mean, then, Sheriff?"

"Sensible means that I travel with you."

"Oh, no you will not. I do not travel with men."

"You will this time," he said. "I'm taking you to Gillette Springs."

Fernanda held up the clothes he'd brought with obvious delight. Jeans, boys' shirts—one red, one blue—and boots and hats. Dreadful hats, like cowboys wore.

"I will not wear those garments!" Caroline announced.

"Yes, you will," he countered. His voice sounded rusty, as if he didn't talk much. Which was probably true, considering his manners.

"*Si*, we will wear them," Fernanda chirruped. She held up the red-checked shirt. "This one for me."

The man called Hawk nodded. "Now, listen up, ladies. Here's what we're going to do."

Chapter Three

At eight o'clock sharp the stagecoach to Gillette Springs rattled up to the Smoke River Hotel and clattered to a stop in a cloud of dust. The driver climbed down and clomped up the steps and through the doorway, emerging a few moments later with a lady's travel trunk over one shoulder. He lashed it on top, then ostentatiously tramped around to lean in the window.

"That all, miss?"

With a nod, he climbed back up into the driver's seat and cracked the whip. "Giddap," he yelled, and the contraption, empty of passengers, rattled off down the street.

From the second floor window of the hotel, Hawk stood next to Caroline MacFarlane, watching the dust dissipate in the morning air. He'd stopped the stage driver outside town and explained the ruse he planned; he knew Caroline didn't agree with his idea. Agree, his father's suspenders! Getting her to even look at the boy's duds he'd bought had taken a stern lecture in his best military give-'em-hell voice and a flood of tears and pleading from *Señora* Sobrano. Miss MacFarlane was fighting him every step of the way.

"I'm going on over to the livery stable to bring the horses," he announced.

"Horses! Excuse me, Mr. Rivera, but I expected, well, another conveyance to transport us. Surely you cannot expect us to ride horses to Gillette Springs?"

"I do. You *do* ride, don't you, miss?"

"Well of course I ride," she retorted. "Every well-bred lady in Boston learns how to ride. What a ridiculous question."

"*Señora* Sobrano?"

Fernanda's smooth olive-skinned face lit up. *"Si,"* she said with obvious relish. "I ride since I was a girl in Mexico."

"Then get dressed, both of you. Meet me at the back kitchen door in twenty minutes. Whoever's tracking you expects you to be on that stage. So, you *won't* be on the stage."

Caroline glowered at him as if he was the devil himself wearing spurs and a badge. She was a helluva lot more attractive without the scowl. He wondered how the even-tempered Fernanda Sobrano had hooked up with her? More than that, how did the older woman put up with this spoiled Boston beauty?

Hawk left them to get ready and went to get the horses. He saddled Red, his black gelding, then picked out two gentle mares for the women and had them saddled, as well.

But when he arrived at the back kitchen door, he got a shock.

Señora Sobrano had turned herself into a reasonable approximation of a somewhat-overweight adolescent boy in jeans and shirt and a pair of store-bought boots. But Caroline Mac-Farlane wouldn't fool a blind man. Her jeans curved enticingly over a nicely rounded bottom, the blue-striped shirt outlined her breasts in no uncertain terms and curly tendrils of dark hair peeked from under the small black Stetson he'd picked out for her.

Hawk groaned aloud.

"What is the matter, Mr. Rivera?" Boston lady's voice was crisp enough to fry bacon and those blue eyes of hers snapped with anger. Goddamn but she was one beautiful hunk of female when she was mad.

"Nothing," he muttered. "Let's mount up." He laced his fingers together for Fernanda, then boosted Caroline up with a splayed hand on her behind.

Big mistake. The bottom part of her anatomy was warm and soft and so female it made his groin swell. God, he didn't need this.

Once mounted, she sat the gray mare so stiff and straight she looked like a ramrod had been shoved up inside her shirt. He tried not to look at her breasts.

"Thought you said you knew how to ride."

"I do know how to ride, but not like this. I ride sidesaddle."

Hawk groaned again. It figured. Not only

that, she looked too elegant. Too starched, somehow.

"Get down," he ordered.

Her eyes widened. "Why should I? I just got up here."

"You don't look right. You're too...clean."

She dismounted so fast he caught his breath, then stalked up to him and propped her hands on her hips. "Too what?" she demanded. "Ladies are supposed to be 'clean.'"

He didn't answer, just scooped up a double handful of dirt and stepped in close. "Don't scream."

He emptied his hands over her shoulders and rubbed the dust in all over her shirt and jeans. Mistake number two. He tried not to register what his fingers were feeling. She hit at him, so he caught her wrist and pinned it while he finished the job.

"Well!" she said when he released her and stepped back out of range. "Now that I look completely disreputable, are you satisfied?"

"Not yet." He snatched off her new-looking hat and crumpled it in both hands, then dropped it onto the ground and stomped his boot on the crown.

When he straightened, Fernanda handed over her hat, as well. He noted she was trying not to laugh. Caroline, however, was looking daggers at him. No sense of humor, he guessed

She struggled up into the saddle by herself this time and Hawk felt a tiny dart of admiration for her resilience. Most women would burst into tears if a man smeared dirt all over them.

He caught his breath as a wayward thought struck home. *Maybe Caroline MacFarlane wasn't like most women.*

Well, hell. He mounted and lifted the reins. "Walk the horses single file. *Señora* Sobrano, you bring up the rear."

"*Si, Señor* Hawk." The smile in her voice told him something he hadn't thought of before. Fernanda Sobrano might be Caroline's valued companion, but she didn't put up with the lady's airs. Or her temper. All at once, the trek to Gillette Springs looked almost enjoyable. At least he wouldn't have to worry about getting bushwhacked. Nobody would expect them to ride the forty miles to Gillette Springs when a stagecoach was available.

They headed south. He hadn't gone five steps before Miss High and Mighty's voice rose in accusation. "Sheriff, we are headed in the wrong direction. Gillette Springs is north of Smoke River, is it not?"

"It is. We're taking a roundabout route, just in case anybody's watching."

That shut her up. He especially liked Fernanda's half-suppressed snort of laughter.

He led them south for a mile, then circled back onto the old river road and eventually headed north on a little-used trail he'd found on an afternoon spent fishing.

The women were quiet for the first couple of hours, and when they stopped to water the horses at a spring, Hawk studied them. Fernanda grinned at him, dismounted and scooped water up in her cupped hands. Caroline tried it but soon gave up.

Hawk thrust his canteen at her. "Here."

She took it without a murmur, tipped the

metal container to her lips and gulped three big swallows. "Tastes awful, like metal," she complained.

"It is metal. It's my old army canteen."

"Oh? Which army, Union or Rebel?"

"I'm a Texan," he said, his voice tight. "Ought to be obvious."

"*Si*, is obvious," Fernanda said from the other side of the spring. "Yankee soldiers not polite like *Señor* Rivera."

Caroline bristled. "There is absolutely nothing wrong with Yankee manners."

"No? *Hija*, your manners could use some improvement sometimes."

Yankee Lady flounced back to her horse and scrambled ungracefully into the saddle. Hawk noticed she was walking a bit stiffly. By sundown she'd be saddle-sore and even more bad tempered. He expelled a long breath. Good thing he'd brought plenty of whiskey.

They stopped before dark in a thick copse of beech and sugar pines. "We stay here?" Fernanda asked.

"Yeah. Gillette Springs is forty miles from

Smoke River. We're almost halfway." He watched the Mexican woman slide easily off her mount. Caroline sat frozen in the saddle, her head drooping.

Hawk didn't ask if she needed help dismounting; he just walked over, snaked his hands around her waist and pulled her off the horse. She staggered, then sagged toward him. He caught her shoulders to keep her upright, but her legs wouldn't support her.

"Fernanda, get a blanket from behind my saddle and spread it over there." He tipped his head toward a patch of thick pine needles.

"Si, señor."

"There's some liniment in my saddlebag. Bring that, too."

The older woman nodded. When she'd spread out the blanket, Hawk scooped Caroline up in his arms.

"Put me down this instant," she cried.

He gritted his teeth. "Unless you want to crawl to that blanket, just shut up." He knelt and rolled her onto the square of Navaho wool, then sat back on his heels.

"Listen, Miss MacFarlane. I didn't want to come along on this trip. I don't want to be here now, soft-talking you into behaving like a civilized person. So unless you want to take your chances alone in the middle of this woods, shape the hell up!"

He waited for a response, then lowered his voice so only she could hear. "From now on, you say please and thank you and act like a lady. You get my meaning?"

She nodded and Hawk saw that tears glistened in her eyes. Well, damn. He rose quickly and tramped over to his horse. He couldn't stand a woman's tears.

Fernanda found the jar of liniment and held it up with a question in her eyes.

"Smear it on her backside," he instructed. "And her thighs," he added. To take his mind off Caroline's anatomy, he busied himself unsaddling and feeding the horses, then dug a hole for the fire so it couldn't be seen and started to unpack supper from his saddlebag.

It didn't help one bit hearing Caroline's responses to the Mexican woman's ministrations with the liniment. "Oh, that feels so good. Do some more, here. And here."

Hawk tried to close his mind off from her voice, but she moaned and sighed like a cat in heat. "Ah, yes, right there. Yes! Oh. *Oh*. More."

He swore under his breath and walked away from camp. When he returned an hour later, Fernanda was grinding coffee beans. Caroline limped over with the coffeepot she'd filled at the stream. Hawk lifted it out of her hands so she wouldn't have to bend over.

"Thank you," she murmured. She wouldn't look at him, but her voice sounded like she'd been crying. He caught his breath. Sure was glad she couldn't see his face in the dark.

While they ate the simple supper of canned beans and tomatoes and hot coffee, he found himself watching her. She sat slumped against a boulder, her knees bent, obviously trying not to move much. He figured her back was aching in spite of the liniment.

What the hell was a delicate slip of an over-civilized woman like Caroline MacFarlane doing traipsing around the country making people mad enough to want her dead?

Tomorrow, he'd ask her. That is, if she was still speaking to him after today.

Chapter Four

My lady very angry today. I think is
because riding on horseback make her
hurt. She is frightened, but she not admit.
Señor Rivera say nothing, not even *bue-
nos días*, until he drink three cups of the
coffee I make extra strong. And I listen to
my lady complain about everything, the
blanket she sleep in, the boots, the biscuits he make for our supper, everything.
She is mad, I think, because underneath
she feel scared.

Caroline had never felt so miserable in her
entire life, not even the hours spent in dusty
stagecoaches rattling through the wilds of

Oklahoma and Texas. She was hot and sticky and her derriere hurt as if she'd been bouncing for hours on a pincushion. A pincushion made of hard leather.

It was all the fault of that odious man, Rivera. He was bossy. Rude. And ill-mannered. No matter how admiringly Fernanda gazed at the tall sheriff, the man was nothing but a bully with a shiny silver badge.

With distaste she surveyed their sleeping arrangements for the night. A single blanket apiece and a saddle for a pillow? How primitive. Even the Indians slept in tents, did they not?

Fernanda had taken the tin plates and spoons to rinse off in the stream; when she returned Caroline would ask her to hold up a blanket so she could undress in what limited privacy she could manage. She wondered with a stab of unease whether she would be able to get her boots off without bending over.

Rivera strode off to hobble the horses and she seized her chance. "Fernanda, hold up one of those blankets to make a screen, would you?"

"But you don't need—"

"Just do it," she hissed. "Quickly! Before he gets back."

Her companion sent her an odd look but dutifully unrolled a square of striped wool and held it aloft. Caroline stepped behind it and started to undo her shirt.

"Hold it!" An unwelcome male voice stopped her midbutton.

"I am undressing, Mr. Rivera. Turn your back. Please," she added as an afterthought. She couldn't stand the thought that he would laugh at her. But the truth was she was, well, frightened. She didn't know how to behave in a camp out in the wilderness with a man nearby.

"Not so fast. Out here on the trail we sleep in our clothes."

"You may do just that, sir. I, however, will not."

Before she could slip free one more button, he yanked the blanket out of Fernanda's upraised hands and tossed it onto the bed of pine needles behind him.

"You hard of hearing? I said out here—"

"I heard you perfectly well. The question is, did *you* hear *me*?" She couldn't continue undressing until he turned away. Caroline pressed her lips together and waited.

"Button yourself back up, lady. You're gonna sleep fully clothed."

"I—I cannot." She would not let him see how uncertain she felt about sleeping out in the open. Next to a man. Most of all, she could not confess that her stiff denim jeans chafed the inside of her thighs, despite the liniment Fernanda had rubbed on earlier. Or that her sunburned neck smarted under her shirt collar. She needed to be free of anything that rubbed her skin.

"Like hell," he muttered. The next thing she knew he had yanked her up like a sack of meal and dumped her onto the blanket closest to the fire pit.

"Ouch!"

He knelt next to her. "I'll take off your boots

so you won't have to stretch. Give me your foot." He turned his back, straddled her leg and began pulling off the leather boots.

How humiliating! With her foot in his control she could not wriggle away from him. Oh, she felt so out of place in the West. So incompetent. She hated not knowing how to do something as simple as taking off her own boots.

But the relief she felt when her boot came off overcame her urge to complain. Bliss! She flexed her toes and closed her eyes with pleasure.

"I think my boots are too small," she said. "My heels are rubbed raw."

"Not too small," he countered. "They're too big. That's why they rub." He took her foot in both hands and stripped off her sock.

"Blisters," he muttered. "Hot damn."

"Well it isn't *my* fault," she blurted out. "You were the one who insisted on horses. And boots."

"Yeah, I did. Stop complaining. You're alive, aren't you?"

"Well!" She had never met a man so bad tempered and prone to give orders. She'd bet he'd been at least a colonel in the Rebel army. Maybe even a general.

"Fernanda," he said over his shoulder to her companion. "You have an extra pair of socks with you?"

"*Si*. I have extra." She rummaged in the small canvas bag he had allowed them and pulled out another bulky pair of boy's socks.

"Your boots fit okay, *señora*?" he asked.

"*Si*." To demonstrate Fernanda executed a few dance steps, snapping her fingers over her head. "Fine boots, *señor. Gracias*."

Caroline's mouth fell open. She had never, ever seen Fernanda dance. Or even walk fast. Even in Texas, when Mama had hired the Mexican woman as a nurse, she had been the epitome of decorum. What had come over her?

That man, Rivera, had come over her, that's what. Caroline sensed some unspoken connection between Rivera and Fernanda, but she could not imagine what it was. He was at least ten years Fernanda's junior, and unless he preferred older women...

How reprehensible! The man was surely taking advantage of her friend.

She tried to yank her foot away, but his big hands held her fast. He massaged her toes, then her arch, and finally drew on the extra sock. Then he picked up her other foot and pulled off the leather boot.

"Tomorrow I'll help you get your boots back on," he said in a matter-of-fact voice.

"There is absolutely no need," she protested. "I have been capable of dressing myself since I was three years old."

"Did you wear Western boots when you were three years old?"

She flinched. "Certainly not. I wore dresses, like any proper young girl."

Without a word he dropped her foot, folded the boot tops over and slapped them down next to her saddle. "Good night, Miss MacFarlane. Use your boots for a pillow."

"*Good night?* How am I supposed to sleep

with just one blanket and a smelly pair of boots?"

He towered over her, then squatted on his haunches down to her level. "You sleep any way you like, Miss MacFarlane. You roll yourself up in the blanket, like a pancake. Personally, I prefer using my saddle as a pillow, but you suit yourself."

She glared up at him. "I most certainly will not roll myself—"

He said nothing, just straightened to his full height and looked down at her. His eyes did strange things to her equilibrium.

"What if I get cold during the night?"

"You won't. It's the middle of the summer. Stays hot all night."

"Oh." Again she stuffed down the unwelcome feeling of incompetence. She should have deduced that about the weather.

"Do not worry, *mi corazón*, you will be close to the fire."

Caroline bit her lip, hunkered down on the blanket, and pulled both corners up around her. Roll over like a pancake? How did one accomplish that?

She rolled to her left and felt the muscles in her back clench. She reversed direction, but the blanket wouldn't cover her completely.

All at once the blanket was yanked out from under her and a hand settled on her backside. "Like this." He tucked one edge under her back and rolled her over twice. The blanket snugged up tight around her body.

"Just like a tortilla," Fernanda chortled. "*Mi hija*, pretend you are the *molé* sauce."

In the next moment he slid his palm under her neck and stuffed her folded boots underneath her head. She clamped her jaw tight shut and watched Fernanda toe off her boots and roll herself up in her own blanket.

Rivera did the same. She noticed he had positioned both herself and Fernanda next to the fire; he slept on the outside.

Well, at least *that* was gentlemanly.

Hawk listened to the quiet breathing of the two women and hoped he'd dropped enough dry wood into the fire pit to last the night. Not that they'd need the warmth, but the flames would keep away predators. He drew in a careful breath. Coyotes, maybe. Not men.

He'd scouted the area around the camp and found no tracks but Red's and those of the two mares. Maybe Fernanda was wrong about someone trying to kill Miss MacFarlane.

He closed his eyes and tried not to remember how Caroline MacFarlane looked with her shirt half-unbuttoned. A song sparrow twittered among the branches of a nearby alder. Funny how a bird's singing could fill a man full of questions about his life. He wondered if his deathbed reflections about the decisions he'd made in his life would make it all clear someday. Then he snorted. He'd save his deathbed confession for when the time came.

He opened his eyes and looked up at the fat silver globe of a moon floating above the trees. Suddenly something startled the bird into silence, and the hair on his neck rose. He hadn't heard a horse. Hadn't heard a single footstep. Very slowly he sat up and reached for his rifle.

A shadow glided behind a thick pine trunk and he thumbed back the hammer. What would a man on foot be doing twenty miles from the nearest town? Maybe a renegade Indian, looking for food?

Or it might be that someone had trailed them, left his mount a mile or so back and sneaked up on the camp.

He got to his feet and crept forward toward the tree. If it was a man intent on harming someone, he'd bet that someone was not himself. Those who held grudges against him he'd left back in Texas, and besides, too much time had passed since his Ranger days. A Mescalero would have caught up with him by now.

He walked to within arm's length of the pine, dug a pebble from his shirt pocket and tossed it off to one side. Nothing, not even an indrawn breath. He chanced a deliberately noisy step onto a dry twig. Still nothing. Then he moved so he could see what was behind the trunk.

Nothing but moonlight and tall trees. Either his imagination was working too hard or he was getting jumpy with two females on his hands. Or…

Then he heard the far-off thud of hoof-beats, and his blood ran cold. Someone had been here. On foot, and so quiet there hadn't been even a warning nicker from the horses. He should have heard something. Anything. God, was he getting old?

He released the hammer, stalked back into camp and dropped the Winchester next to his bedroll.

"Señor?"

"It was nothing, Fernanda. Go back to sleep."

"You lie, my friend. I hear the horse, too."

"You've got good ears, *señora.*"

"Ay, that is true." There was a long pause and then the Mexican woman's soft voice spoke again. "I have learned to listen, *señor.*"

Hawk didn't sleep. He didn't even try, just lay awake with his thoughts and his doubts and his fears. Not for himself, but for the spir-ited, headstrong crusader who slept a short distance away from him. She was a damn fool of a woman, sticking her nose where it didn't belong.

But he'd agreed to protect her, and he would. Stealthily he moved his bedroll as close to hers as he could get without waking her.

Tomorrow he'd teach her how to shoot his revolver.

"*Señora*, can you fire a pistol?"

"*Sí.*"

"A pistol!" Caroline spluttered.

"*Sí.* I carry a *pistola* always in my pocket."

"What?" Her voice rose an octave. "Fernanda, you never told me that."

"You never ask, *mi corazón*. Besides, I never tell you lots of things."

Caroline struggled to her feet and immediately regretted it. Her legs felt stiff as new sofa springs. Nevertheless, she marched over to Fernanda, who sat placidly beside the fire pit eating the last of the biscuits. Before she could confront the Mexican woman, Rivera laid his big hand on Caroline's shoulder and spun her toward him so fast it made her dizzy.

"There's something I want to show you before we get started."

"Oh? And what is that, Mr. Rivera? How to take off my boots, perhaps?"

A smile flickered. The first hint of any humor in the taciturn sheriff and a welcome change from that smoldering anger in his green eyes and the perpetual frown he wore. My goodness, what a sourpuss he was. He'd be nice-looking if his face were not so scrunched up.

"Nothing to do with boots," he said in that maddeningly calm voice of his. Didn't he ever get excited about anything? Even Fernanda's impromptu fandango last night hadn't cracked his impassive expression. He must have been a superb soldier in the War, imperturbable as a sphinx under fire.

She sniffed. "Well, what is it? Show me and let us be on our way. I have a speaking engagement in Gillette Springs this evening."

He shot her a look. "I want you to learn to use a revolver."

She sucked in a breath. "I beg your pardon?

What on earth for?" The very thought of putting her hand on a firearm sent a shudder up her spine. Did women out West actually do such brazen things?

"For protection."

"Yours or mine? No well-bred lady handles firearms."

"No well-bred lady travels out West lighting fires under half the population without knowing how to protect herself."

"Lighting fires? Well, I should hope so. For your information, Mr. Rivera, 'lighting fires' is going to be the salvation of womankind."

He said nothing, just took hold of her upper arm and propelled her away from the fire. Fernanda fled to the stream with the empty tin cups and the coffeepot.

He slid his revolver out of the holster on his hip, spilled the chambered bullets into his palm and thrust the weapon at her, holding it by the blued steel barrel. She knocked it out of his hand onto the ground.

His eyes narrowed into glittery emerald slits. "Pick it up," he ordered.

"I can't. I am too stiff to bend over."

"Then you shouldn't have dropped the gun. I said pick it up." He put one hand at her waist and the other at her back and jackknifed her body. She groaned through gritted teeth.

"Pick it up," he repeated.

She scrabbled on the ground and managed to grab the long barrel, but it was heavier than she expected. She couldn't lift it with one hand.

"Use two hands," he ordered.

She pushed the weapon toward her other hand and grasped the handle.

"Now straighten up." He bit the words out like firecrackers going off.

"You got me doubled over like this," she said. "*You* can get me to straighten up."

Too late she realized her mistake. He slapped one hand on her midsection, grasped her shoulder with the other and yanked her upright.

Her muscles screamed and she wanted to weep with frustration. She thought about stamping her foot onto his toe, but she knew she couldn't lift it high enough.

"Now," he instructed, positioning her hand on the gun. "Fold your fingers around the butt and slip your forefinger onto the trigger." He laid his hand over hers and curled her fingers over the handle. She couldn't hold up the weight, and the barrel drooped toward the ground.

"You right-handed?" When she nodded, he grabbed her left hand and pressed her fingers on the opposite side. "Hold it steady."

"I am trying! It is too heavy for a woman."

"Not too heavy for a crusader," he said drily.

She glanced into his face. "You think I am a crusader?"

"Hell, yes." He stepped behind her, brought both hands around her body and rested them under her forearms to steady her grip.

She didn't like the feel of him at her back. Or the warmth of his arms around hers. Or anything. He smelled of leather and wood smoke and sweat. Well, she acknowledged, she probably smelled the same. He didn't seem to mind, because he moved his jaw right up against her hair.

"Breathe in," he said. "Now breathe out."

She couldn't. Not with him so close. Not without revealing how uneven her breathing had become all of a sudden.

He lifted her forearms and the gun barrel leveled off parallel to the ground. "Now sight down the barrel."

"Sight? What does that mean, 'sight'?"

He snorted. "Hell, lady, it means aim the damn gun!" With his chin he nudged her head down. "Look through those two little notches and point the barrel at something."

She'd like to point it at *him*. Instead she swung the weapon toward a low-hanging branch.

"Now squeeze the trigger."

She heard a metallic snap.

"Good. Now we'll try it with a bullet."

Patiently Hawk showed her how to crack open the chamber and slide the cartridges into the slots. She was a quick study, and that surprised him. He only had to show her something once. She was obviously intelligent. Probably had attended some fancy girls' school, maybe even college.

When she'd loaded his revolver he instructed her about not swinging the barrel around but keeping it pointed down, then showed her how to release the hammer.

"Okay, now aim at something." Hawk stepped in behind her again and watched her point the weapon at another tree branch.

"Try not to hit a bird," he joked. She didn't even crack a smile. "Don't wait too long or your hands will start to shake."

"My hands are already shaking," she said. Her voice was shaking, as well.

"Bring the barrel up slowly. Now hold your breath and sight. When you're ready, just squeeze back on the trigger."

The revolver discharged with a sharp crack, and the kick propelled her backward into his chest. Instinctively he grabbed her shoulders. "A gun always pushes back when you fire it, so you need to be ready."

He liked holding her that way, her backbone pressed against his chest. Her head just fit under his chin. Damn, her hair smelled good, like lemons and some kind of soap.

He could feel every breath she took and he wasn't liking his reaction one bit. He wanted to slide his fingers around to her chest, cup her breasts and feel her heart beat under his thumb.

He snatched his hands away so fast it was as if a bee had stung him. Now, that was an interesting reaction.

No, it was a damn worrisome reaction. He didn't have time to dally with a woman, especially this woman, all proper and educated and remote.

Even more important, he didn't have the guts for it. Not anymore.

Chapter Five

They arrived in Gillette Springs just as the sun dipped behind the mountains to the north. The trunk sat waiting in the hotel foyer, as Hawk had instructed, so he arranged for a room. The women ordered a bathtub to be brought up. He made sure they bolted the door and strode off to find the sheriff.

The man's office was just three doors down from the hotel, but nobody was there. A sign stuck to the door read At Polly's Cage. Back at five.

Good idea. He could use a shot of whiskey before heading back.

"Sheriff Davis in town?"

The pie-eyed deputy leaned against the polished wood bar and sent Hawk a sloppy grin. "Leadin' a posse up to Idaho," the paunchy man allowed with a derisive snort. "Left me in charge, he did. In charge of what, I'd like to know. Nuthin' exciting ever happens in this town."

"Might be something exciting tonight," Hawk offered. "Suffragette lady's making a speech."

"Oh, yeah, I heard about her. Over at the church, seven o'clock."

"Listen, Deputy, someone took a shot at the lady two nights ago in Smoke River. Think you should…" Hawk leaned toward him and lowered his voice. Then he stopped short and studied the man. Old. Out of shape. And drunk. This deputy couldn't protect a dog from a flea.

Hell. All he wanted to do was head back to Smoke River and forget the woman now taking a bath at the hotel. He wanted to get as far away as possible from Caroline MacFarlane.

But he couldn't leave her to the protection of this sorry excuse for a lawman. He ground his teeth until his jaw hurt.

"How about you make sure nobody sits down in that church tonight without removing their sidearms. Pile 'em up on the back pew and guard them."

"Oh. Oh, sure, mister. I'll do that for sure."

And not much else, Hawk realized. The minute Caroline entered the church she would be a sitting pigeon. Hell and damn, he couldn't leave her. When he returned to Smoke River he'd send off a stiff note to Sheriff Davis about his derelict deputy, but for tonight, Hawk figured he'd have to stand in. Maybe he'd have to rethink the whole thing to keep this headstrong woman safe.

He grabbed a bath and a shave at the barbershop across the street from the saloon, then went up the hotel stairs to tell Fernanda and Caroline what not to do tonight.

"Whatever do you mean, don't wear this dress? This is my most tailored suit. It is perfectly proper and stylish and it commands resp—"

"It makes you look stiff and superior and men hate women like that."

Caroline drew herself up as tall as she could and glared at him. "Oh, they do, do they? Well, let me tell you something. It is not *men* I am trying to reach, Mr. Rivera. It is the *women* I want to hear my message."

"No, it isn't. It's the men you need to convince. The women are already on your side."

Fernanda laid a restraining hand on her arm. "He is right, *hija*. It is men who will be voting to give the vote to the women."

Rivera yanked open the door to her wardrobe where she'd hung up her dresses and flicked through the hangers. "Wear something frilly," he said. "Something with ruffles or bows or ribbons or something." He pulled out her flounced yellow skirt.

"Wear this."

"That is meant for a party or a reception. It is entirely too dressy for speech-making."

"Wear it anyway."

The man was impossible. She eyed his selection with trepidation. It was entirely too frivolous for playing the role of a—what had he called her?—a crusader?

Oh, Mama, I am beginning to wish I had known more about what I would be getting into.

But Fernanda had a point; it *was* men who would be voting to change the suffrage law.

"I—I cannot do it. I refuse to…to…well, seduce the men with a pretty dress."

"You want to win the war," he grumbled, "you do what you have to do." He reached over and plucked the pins holding her bun at her neck.

"And wear your hair down."

She gasped as her hair tumbled free. "Just what do you think you are doing?"

"Damned if I know," he muttered. "Keeping you safe. Out of the line of fire from some crazy gent who wants to stop you."

"Oh." The look on his face stopped every protest she could think of.

"Look, Caroline," he said. "I don't believe in your cause. I don't want you women to win the vote. But I also don't want you to get yourself killed."

"Oh," she said again. Suddenly all the air whooshed out of her and all her brave words dissolved into thin air. Very well, she would do it. She would wear the yellow dress. She would be soft and feminine and she would win the vote of the men on behalf of the women. Rivera was right. It was exactly like going to war.

But oh, Lord, no one had told her how frightening it could be.

"Get dressed," Hawk ordered. "I'll walk you to the church in ten minutes." Like a good soldier, she didn't even flinch. Made him wonder something else about her.

He closed the door and paced up and down the carpeted hallway outside and tried to figure her out.

The church was filled to overflowing. The mix of seated men and women was about even. Deputy Saunders had secured all the sidearms on the back pew and was standing guard over the pile of holsters and gun belts and revolvers. At least he had sobered up.

Hawk had arranged with the minister to use

the entrance in back of the pulpit so Caroline would not have a long walk up the aisle. Fernanda was already seated in the front pew, her face looking serene and her hands folded in her lap. But her dark eyes were wide with apprehension.

Caroline stood next to him, waiting for the last of her audience to squeeze into a pew. She took his breath away in that yellow dress. Hell, she'd have every man in the church in love with her before she even opened her mouth.

She, too, looked calm. Resolute. Suffused with soldierly purpose. He'd seen lieutenants with less steel in their spine.

She also looked female as hell and too vulnerable. His chest tightened just a fraction more than he liked.

Beside him, she drew in a shaky breath and started forward.

"Wait." He laid his hand at her waist and pulled her to a stop beside him, then slipped the small pistol he'd bought out of his vest and pressed it into her hand.

"What is this?" she whispered.

"It's a pistol. It's lighter than my revolver. Carry it in your skirt pocket."

"I—"

"Careful," he said. He closed her fingers around the gun butt. "It's loaded."

She snatched her hand away, then nodded. "Thank you." He watched her slip it into her pocket.

"Ready? Let's go."

As he had instructed, she moved through the doorway and quickly placed herself behind the minister's solid oak lectern. Hawk followed, seated himself on a side chair just behind the pulpit, and scanned the crowd. Quietly he laid his revolver across his lap.

The audience couldn't see the weapon; besides, every eye was glued to the vision in yellow standing at the front of the church.

"Ladies and gentlemen, my name is Caroline MacFarlane." She kept her voice low and even, not a hint of harangue or inflammatory words. Good girl.

"I want to tell you about my mother, Evangeline MacFarlane. When I was old enough to notice such things, I became aware that my—" she hesitated and Hawk tensed "—my father struck my mother. He did this often, almost every night, and he made no attempt to hide from me what he was doing."

She paused and Hawk focused on the men in the crowd. Some looked angry; some looked a little guilty; but most bore a look of concern.

"When I was twelve years old my mother took me away from our home. She said she could not live like that any longer, and no matter how my father begged and pleaded, she refused to go back."

The women in the audience nodded and murmured to each other. A few even dabbed at their eyes.

"But my father went to court. And the judge—" Again she stopped and this time she swallowed hard. "The judge said my mother had to return to my father, had to live with him even though he mistreated her. He said it was the law in Massachusetts, that if a woman left her husband, she forfeited her right to her children."

Hawk studied the faces of the men. No doubt some of them beat their wives. Maybe they felt they were justified; maybe a few felt guilty. But not one of them challenged Caroline or shouted an insult. Instead, they waited to hear her next words.

"My mother decided this was wrong, that forcing a woman to live with an abusive husband was wrong. She moved us into a room at a boardinghouse. Later, to save herself—and me—she left him for good and took me with her. She joined a group of women and spoke out against this injustice, and other injustices against women. We traveled all over the country, and everywhere we went, my mother spoke out to support women."

In the uneasy silence, Hawk finally began to breathe easier. It was not an unruly crowd; the men were stirred up, he could see that, but they weren't violent.

Caroline went on, her voice still soft. "Did you know that here in Oregon a woman cannot divorce a man for cruelty or abandonment? And that if a woman earns any money of her own, it goes to her husband?"

She paused again. "Ladies and gentlemen, do you think this is fair?"

There was a sudden commotion at the back of the church. Hawk lifted his revolver, shielding it from view with his hand, and thumbed back the hammer. But the cause of the disturbance was a young boy of about eight or nine, who darted up the aisle to where Caroline stood and thrust a folded piece of paper into her hand.

"Man said to give you this," he panted.

She unfolded the note and gasped. Then she looked over at Hawk.

Her face had gone white as milk.

Chapter Six

Hawk didn't much care what the note said, but it told him Caroline's speech was over. He lifted his Colt and stepped past her. "That's all, folks. Miss MacFarlane just got some bad news and she has to leave."

Behind him he heard the paper rustle and knew her hand was shaking. He ached to turn back to her, but he couldn't take his eyes off the crowd.

The church began to empty. Women chattered excitedly to each other, the men picked up their sidearms under Deputy Saunders's watchful gaze and went out.

Fernanda edged past him and reached out

to Caroline. "*Mi corazón*, you look like ghost. *Que pasa?*"

Finally the last man left, followed by the deputy, and Hawk reholstered his revolver. The Mexican woman stood patting Caroline's trembling hands, her face bleached of color. She held the note out to him. "Here, *señor*. You read."

Hawk had the sinking feeling that the contents were going to tie him into something he wanted no part of. Long ago he'd learned to watch his back when something didn't feel right, and this sure didn't feel right.

He glanced at the paper Fernanda had stuffed into his hand. Crudely printed in red crayon were the words "I WILL GET YOU BITCH."

He looked up to find Caroline staring at him like she'd been poleaxed, her widened eyes darkening to blue-violet and her mouth clamped shut so tight her lips formed a thin unsmiling slash in her pale face.

He stepped forward and laid his arm around her shoulders.

"D-don't," she whispered. "I need to be strong."

He could feel her whole body shaking. "Don't be a fool. You need to stop trying to be brave."

She jerked her head up. "Don't tell me what to do! If I p-pretend, it gives me courage. I grew up pretending."

Hawk snorted. "Someone just threatened your life, Caroline. You should be damn scared, not playacting."

Fernanda nodded emphatically. "Always she pretend."

Suddenly Hawk wanted to fold her into his arms, but he figured that would frighten her even more. He settled for tightening his arm about her shoulders and gently tugging her toward the doorway behind the pulpit.

"Come on. You need to go back to the hotel and lie down. Maybe have some coffee brought up."

"I n-need something stronger than coffee." Her voice was less shaky, but she was still trembling like she'd taken a bad chill. He guided her to the back entrance, but before stepping through the door he pulled her to a stop.

"Wait." He withdrew his revolver and inched out the doorway far enough to see both sides of the street. Not a sign of a living soul. A faint light shone in the window of the sheriff's office, but no horses were tied at the hitching rail in front of Polly's Cage. Tinny piano music drifted from the saloon. He moved to the corner and studied the buildings on both sides of the main street—still nothing.

He stepped back inside. "Looks clear."

Caroline drew a deep breath and started forward, but Hawk reached out and yanked her close to his side, then motioned to the Mexican woman hovering behind him. "Fernanda, stay on the other side of her."

"Si, señor." She grasped Caroline's arm.

Once inside the hotel Hawk lifted his arm from Caroline's slim shoulders, grabbed the room key and went up the stairs ahead of her, his revolver drawn. He unlocked the door, checked inside the wardrobe and under both beds. Fernanda hurried to close the curtains and then confronted him. "What we do now, *señor*?"

Damned if he knew. He couldn't leave Caroline alone with just Fernanda; even if the Mexican woman did carry a pistol, he'd bet she wasn't experienced, and Caroline...

Caroline needed a shot of Dutch courage. Hell, he needed one, too. He also needed to think. He made sure the women were safe and had locked the door. Then he walked over to the sheriff's office for some reconnaissance and on to Polly's Cage for some comfort.

By the time Rivera returned, Caroline had talked her fear down to a manageable level and explained again to Fernanda that, no matter what, she would not stop making speeches. She would never stop.

She was afraid, yes. Whoever it was had managed to track her down, and sending a child with such an awful note, in front of everyone, had chilled her to the bone. But she could never let it show. And yes, she used her stiff, proper manners to disguise the terror, the fear that she actually *would* be killed. Her life, speaking out about what had happened to her mother, and to her, compelled her to go on, even when her heart hammered under her buttons and her throat was so dry she could not spit.

Oh, Mama, if you are looking down on me, give me courage, for I know I must go on.

She had just donned her silk night robe when she heard Rivera's voice on the other side of the door. Fernanda stopped brushing her hair, turned the key in the lock and let him in.

In his hand he carried three glasses and a pint of whiskey.

Fernanda reached for the bottle. "Ah, *señor*, you are an angel from God."

"Not quite," he growled. "I talked with the deputy sheriff. That kid was the barber's son. He'd never seen the man who gave him the note. No horse that he could see, but the fellow was tall. Spare build. Walked hunched over a bit. Dark clothing and a hat pulled too low to see his face."

Fernanda poured three glasses of whiskey. "What we do now, *señor*?"

Hawk slapped his hat down on the bed nearest the door and downed a big swallow of the liquor. "You're not gonna like this any more than I do, but—" he took another gulp "—I'm sticking to you like cockleburs on a horse's tail."

Caroline sank onto the other bed and eyed him. "I beg your pardon? What exactly does that mean?"

She was dressed for bed, Hawk noted. Bare feet, her hair a loose tangle of curls. For an instant he lost his train of thought.

"It means I'm sleeping in your room tonight. It means you do exactly as I say until I can get you to wherever you're going next."

"Boise. In Idaho. We plan to catch the train from Oakridge."

"That's fifty miles from here."

"There's a stagecoach tomorrow morning."

He thought that over. Maybe the stage would be safer than traveling on horseback, especially since whoever was trailing them, if anybody really *was* trailing them, apparently hadn't been fooled.

A suffocating sense of duty descended on him, the kind of obligation he swore he'd never undertake again. But hell's bells, here he was, up to his neck in it again. He prayed to God it would turn out better this time.

He polished off his whiskey and poured another for himself and for Fernanda. Caroline had wrinkled her nose at her first sip and the glass she now rotated in her two hands was still full.

"Okay, tomorrow we take the stagecoach to Oakridge." And he'd pray every mile that the sheriff in Boise was not holed up in a saloon or out with a posse chasing some outlaw. He wouldn't relax until both women were safe inside the hotel.

Before first light, Hawk arranged with the livery owner to board Red and the two mares, then walked over to the sheriff's office, where he caught the deputy asleep at his desk. The man was damn incompetent, but at least he listened and agreed to keep his mouth shut. By eight, Hawk had taken the stage driver aside and explained some things while the women climbed on board.

"Ya wanna ride shotgun, Hawk?"

He thought it over. Jingo could probably use an extra rifle, so he nodded and stepped around to explain to Fernanda and Caroline. "Going to be a long trip, ladies, but we'll be stopping in Tumbleweed for fresh horses and some dinner."

The two women nodded, but neither was in a smiling frame of mind. Couldn't blame them one bit. He climbed up beside the driver and laid his Winchester across his lap. "All set, Jingo. Let's go."

Jingo released the brake and lifted his whip, but before he could snap it over the team, a tall man barreled down the hotel steps and yanked open the passenger door. "Aw, hell." Jingo spit a mouthful of tobacco juice beside the coach.

Hawk grabbed his rifle but Jingo laid a gnarled hand on the barrel.

"You know that guy?" Hawk asked.

"Sorta. Gambler sometimes. Horse trader other times." The whip cracked and the stage lurched forward.

"Is he on any Wanted posters?"

"Naw. Too slippery if ya ask me. S'ides, gambling ain't illegal. Yet."

"Yet? What does that mean?"

Jingo spat again. "Women get the vote, first thing them straitlaced old biddies'll do is outlaw card playing."

Hawk kept his mouth shut about the passengers and the straitlaced part. Sure was thought-stopping, though. He'd once won a woman in a card game.

He couldn't help worrying about what was going on inside the coach. Couldn't hear anything over the thunder of horses' hooves and creaking wheels. He knew Fernanda would fire off a shot if something was wrong, but...

"Hold up, Jingo."

"Huh? What for?"

"You heard me, pull up."

He was off the driver's bench before the

stage rattled to a stop. He strode around to the passenger door and yanked it open.

Fernanda let out a screech. "What happen, *señor*?"

"Nothing, yet. Any trouble back here?"

Caroline sat straight-backed in her severe dark blue dress, her hands primly folded in her lap. Hawk noted her knuckles were white. Gambler man tipped his black derby back off his face and blinked small round eyes at him. "You expecting some trouble, Sheriff?"

Hawk swore under his breath. The man was sprawled beside Fernanda, his long legs resting on the seat next to Caroline. Hawk used the rifle barrel to knock them to the floor.

"Hey, what the—?"

"You only paid for one seat, mister. The one next to the lady doesn't belong to you."

"Oh, very well. Excuse me, ma'am." The watery eyes closed and he tipped the derby back over his face. Caroline sent Hawk a grateful look.

"You all right?" he mouthed.

The ghost of a smile curved her lips and

she nodded. Hawk tipped his head toward the stranger and lifted his eyebrows in a question. Again she smiled, and this time it touched her eyes.

He sucked in air as his stomach rolled over, then latched the door and rejoined Jingo on the driver's bench.

"Them ladies all right?"

He grunted.

"Relax, Hawk. We got some hard hours on the road ahead of us."

"You just drive this contraption, Jingo." He wouldn't relax until they reached Oakridge. But he couldn't stop thinking about Gambling Man inside the coach, whether he was really on the up-and-up or whether he flimflammed when he saw a badge.

Sweat began at the back of his neck. Another few hours of this and he'd draw his weapon on every male that came within twenty feet of her.

"Ya want me to sing somethin'?" Jingo quipped. "The horses like it when I sing."

Hawk rolled his eyes.

Jingo warbled in an off-tune tenor voice all

the way to the stage station. By the time they pulled up at the small two-room shack, Hawk's patience was wearing thinner than the film on a stagnant frog pond.

Chapter Seven

Caroline stepped down onto the ground and grabbed for Fernanda's steadying hand. Her legs were stiff, a headache pounded in her temples and her bottom was numb from hours and hours perched on the hard leather bench. Behind them, the man who'd introduced himself as Mr. Overby jerked awake and snuffled. "Ah, dinner," he exclaimed.

She doubted she could eat anything after jouncing along in the stifling heat but she could surely drink something; her throat was dry and scratchy as sandpaper. And her nerves were jumpy.

Fernanda conducted her into the tiny station, asked for water and walked on through straight to the necessary. When they returned, their host, a grizzled old man with a greasy apron looped around his waist, showed them to a rough wood table and dished up bowls of what looked like stew. Caroline picked up her spoon and immediately set it down and pushed the bowl away.

"You must eat, *mi corazón*. We have many miles ahead."

She couldn't. Caroline drank glass after glass of water, but her stomach was too unsettled for food. She watched Mr. Overby shovel in huge mouthfuls of his meal until he looked up.

"What are you staring at, miss?"

Caroline jerked. "Nothing." She turned her gaze away and Hawk Rivera slid in beside her, bringing with him the scent of leather and sweat. She much preferred it over the cologne-heavy smell of Mr. Overby. In fact she was beginning to like the way the sheriff smelled, like a man instead of a candy shop. She wished he would sit inside the coach with them.

"Stew any good?" he queried.

"I wouldn't know. I cannot eat it."

He snaked out his hand and pulled her bowl back to her. "Try," he ordered. "Making speeches takes strength."

"Do not tell me you like my speeches?" She worked to keep the surprise out of her voice.

He set his tall glass of water onto the table. "No, I don't."

Fernanda looked at him from across the table. "*Que?* You do not like?"

Their driver tramped in through the door. "Aha, supper! Thought I was gonna starve to death afore we got here. Food any good, Hawk?"

"Yeah." He slanted a look at Fernanda. "And no, I do not like the speeches."

Caroline leaned toward him. "Why not?" she intoned.

"Doesn't matter."

"But it does matter," she protested.

"Not to me."

She sat back and sucked in her breath. "Then why are you…? Oh, of course. You are a lawman. An ex-Texas Ranger, Fernanda said. You feel…responsible."

Somehow that made her angry. So angry that without thinking she jammed her spoon into the bowl of stew and swallowed down a bite. Beside her, Rivera dipped his head and chuckled.

Well! At least she had cracked that imperturbable demeanor of his.

"It's true I don't like your speeches," he said in a low voice. "Don't let it bother you."

"What? Of course it bothers me."

He laid down his spoon and looked directly at her. "Why?"

She opened her mouth to respond, then snapped it shut. "Why" was a very good question. She should not care what this man thought of her speeches. Or her ideas. Or her.

"Shouldn't bother you," he reiterated.

"No," she murmured, "it shouldn't. I will address that issue on the remainder of our trip to Oakridge."

"Might do better to get some sleep," he said.

"That," she said crisply, "is difficult."

He resumed eating. "Yeah, probably impossible. Better than riding a horse, though, isn't it?"

She laughed aloud, then clapped her hand over her mouth. "Yes, much better," she said between her fingers.

"Good. You were a disaster on horseback."

She laughed again. "Was I really?"

He shot her a sideways glance. "You were."

He didn't say it unkindly, but it nettled her just the same. Was he always so blunt? All at once she wondered what sort of woman he was used to? What sort of woman did he like?

Fernanda patted her mouth with her wrinkled napkin and stood up. "I go for walk," she announced.

Hawk snagged her forearm as she moved past. "No, you don't, *señora*."

"Ah," she acknowledged after a slight hesitation. "Perhaps I do not."

Hawk grinned up at her. "I do like a smart woman, Fernanda."

He wondered at the odd look that crossed Caroline's face, but before he could puzzle over it, he saw Jingo signaling him from the doorway. He rose, tossed down the sorry excuse for a napkin, and followed the driver outside. Dusk was falling; the big orange sun slipped slowly behind the hills and shadows were lengthening.

"Time to roll, Hawk. Got us about three hours till full dark."

Hawk tried to shrug off the tension that tightened his belly into knots. Darkness was never a good time to avoid danger, especially the kind he sensed dogging the two women under his protection.

He paced twice around the stagecoach and tried to think about the situation he found himself in. A woman like Caroline MacFarlane was always going to be trouble, purposely sticking her pretty little neck out and just begging some lowlife to harm her. As soft and female as she appeared, she had a spine of steel and a stubborn streak wide as a housewife's broom.

But he sure did wish her hands weren't so white, that her voice wasn't low and just throaty enough to sound seductive. That her mouth… Ah, hell, he couldn't think about her mouth. And that hair, like fine spun silk and so black it reminded him of an ebony Arabian he'd lusted after years ago.

He handed his rifle up to Jingo and sat until Caroline and Fernanda walked out of the station and climbed into the coach. Followed half a heartbeat later by Overby.

Hawk eyed him. The gambler might not look menacing, but he sure made Hawk's nerves twitch.

Caroline closed her eyes to avoid Mr. Overby's glassy stare. The stagecoach had set off at a rapid clip and, despite the rough ride, the man had slept until ten minutes ago. Now that it was growing dark outside he suddenly became talkative.

Fernanda sent her a warning glance, and she resolved not to engage in conversation. Like most men, no doubt he was violently opposed to giving women the vote; the less she said the better.

Outside the coach window the landscape

changed from gently rolling golden hills and broad valleys to a high tree-swathed plateau. Pines, Caroline guessed. Dark green, like those at their camp two nights ago, only closer together. Not much grew on the ground beneath them save for a kind of straggly grass with pale yellow flowers. Her lips firmed. The state of Oregon was inhospitable to not only women's rights; green growing things struggled for life, as well.

So Mr. Rivera did not like her speeches, did he? She would say he was a typical male, except that he was not typical at all. She had never known a man even remotely like him. In Texas, the Rangers were famous. And feared. After three days in Rivera's company, she could understand why.

Hawk Rivera rarely smiled, and his disturbing green eyes missed nothing. He had even noticed her choking on the whiskey he'd brought last night and that she did not finish her stew an hour ago.

His skin was tanned to a shade darker than even the stage driver's. Perhaps Rivera was part Mexican? But his given name was Anderson—not a Mexican name. Hawk could be an Indian nickname, a spirit name she'd heard it termed. Yes, that was it. He was like a hawk, predatory and no doubt lethal when crossed.

His voice, however, had no hint of an accent, Mexican or Indian. Though his words were blunt, they were carefully chosen and always to the point. Had he had some schooling, then? Also she couldn't help wondering why he had left Texas.

A shout from the driver jolted her to attention. The coach slowed, then swerved hard to the right. Fernanda jerked awake. "What is happening?"

Hawk spotted something on the road ahead and yelled at Jingo. A tree lay across the trail, fresh cut it looked like.

"I see it," Jingo yelled. He started to slow the team.

"Don't stop, man! Go around it."

The driver manhandled the traces, but with

the trees so thick, there was nowhere to go. The coach veered hard and rattled to a stop.

Ambush? Hawk cocked his rifle, raised it shoulder high and scanned ahead through the deepening gloom.

"See anything?" Jingo breathed.

"No." Still, it was too quiet.

"Think somebody laid that pine down a-purpose?"

"Yeah, I do. We'll have to move it to get past."

"Damn."

"I'll get Overby out here to help." He swung down to the ground.

Hawk had to lay down his Winchester to help the other two men jockey the tree out of the road, but the instant the rifle left his hand, a gunshot rang out. He dropped his end of the log and dove for his weapon, rolled once and fired into the trees, Then he sprinted for the coach.

"Take cover," he yelled. A bullet whanged into the passenger door. Wood splintered, and from inside came Fernanda's answering voice.

"You also, *señor*."

He sighted his weapon into the trees but saw no movement of any kind. If he could force the man to fire again, the flare would pinpoint his location. He edged around the coach, keeping it at his back. If whoever it was wanted Caroline or Fernanda, they'd have to kill him first.

He waited. Out of the corner of his eye he saw Jingo and Overby shove the tree aside, and Jingo scrambled back up into the driver's seat.

"Overby!" Hawk shouted. "Get up there next to him."

The traces jingled softly as Jingo picked them up, and then the stage started to roll forward. Hawk hooked his left hand onto the coach door handle. "Go!" he yelled.

He heard the whip crack and he swung the door open and hung on. Another shot and this one grazed his upper arm. Jingo slowed just enough so he could fling his body inside.

Hands grabbed him. He pulled the rifle in and felt the stage pick up speed. Someone caught the door handle and heaved it shut.

He knew it was the Mexican woman because Caroline was crushed on the floor beneath him.

He lifted his body off her, tossed the rifle down and pounded his fist twice on the roof. He heard Jingo give a Rebel yell and the stage accelerated.

"You are hurt!" Fernanda exclaimed.

"It's minor." It didn't feel minor; it felt like a dull butcher knife had sliced into his skin, but he was alive and they were moving and he'd count his blessings later. He kicked his rifle out of the way and collapsed onto the seat. Then he reached down to help Caroline up off the floor.

"You all right?" he grated.

She nodded and tried to smile. The half-brave, half-terrified expression on her face sent a swift, sweet arrow straight into his gut. She reached out to touch his bloody arm.

"Don't," he cautioned.

She snatched her hand back. "Does it hurt?"

Hell yes, it hurt. "Some, yeah."

Fernanda lifted up her black skirt and ripped

off the bottom ruffle of her petticoat. "Let me, *señor*." She wadded up the pad of cotton and pressed it hard where the blood was oozing. He shoved over on the seat to make room for her.

Fernanda shook her head. "Caroline, you sit next. Press hard where it bleeds."

Caroline turned white, but the Mexican woman took her small manicured hand and slapped her palm against Hawk's shoulder.

"Don't faint," he cautioned.

"I never faint."

"You see a lot of bloody bullet wounds making speeches, do you?"

"Of course not. Who was that shooting at you?"

"Don't know. And I'm betting he wasn't aiming for me. It was you he wanted."

Her hand jerked away from the compress and her face turned even more pasty. "Oh."

"You gonna faint?"

"Certainly not." She slapped the bloody pad back onto his arm. Hawk caught her hand.

"Caroline, you don't have to do this."

She sent him a look with those purple-blue

eyes of hers that stopped his heartbeat. "Oh, yes I do. You are risking your life to protect us."

"Correction, Miss Speech-Maker," he muttered. "You're the one out there stirring up the hornets' nests. It's you I'm protecting."

Caroline said nothing. The truth was she could not think of one single sensible thing to say. And that was not at all like her. For the past year her whole life had been spent saying sensible things.

"Señor," Fernanda said softly, "I am remember you in my prayers."

Rivera looked across at Fernanda, and Caroline swallowed hard. Hawk Rivera's green eyes were suspiciously shiny.

Chapter Eight

The stage pulled up in front of the Excelsior Hotel, on what Hawk would loosely call the main street of the thriving little town of Oakridge. It looked a lot like Smoke River, except there were more storefronts and the boardwalk was wider. Fernanda reached for the coach door, but he laid a restraining hand on her arm.

"I'll go first."

"But you are wounded, *señor*!"

Gently he dislodged Caroline's head from where it lolled against his shoulder and hefted his rifle in his other hand. He hated like anything to disturb her; feeling her body sag against him was the best thing that had happened on this whole miserable trip. But, he thought with regret, he guessed this little patch of peace in the middle of a crazy night had to end.

"Stay put until I come for you." He swung the door open and planted his boots on the ground.

The hotel was lit up like a Christmas tree, light glowing from every window, even from the rooms way up on the top floor. That's where he wanted to be, he decided, up high so he could see both sides of the street.

Jingo began unloading Caroline's trunk, and Overby stumbled down off his perch on the driver's bench and lurched unsteadily down the street toward the Red Rooster Saloon. Hawk waited until Jingo set the trunk inside the hotel foyer, then motioned him to wait and tossed him his Winchester.

"Keep the ladies company. I'll just step into the hotel and get a room."

"Take yer time, Hawk. One of these ladies is real purty."

Hawk halted midstride. "Hands off," he snapped.

Jingo's bushy eyebrows rose. "You claimin' them both?"

"Hell, yes, you randy old buzzard." He strode up the wooden steps with Jingo's half-admiring laughter in his ears.

He had to push the wiry desk clerk a bit and let his vest flap open to show his badge, but he secured a room on the third floor. He waited while the desk clerk and a lanky kid lugged the trunk up the three flights of stairs and by that time he had to admit he was feeling light-headed. He needed food, whiskey and some sleep, in that order.

Once inside the tiny hotel room, Fernanda had other ideas. "You do not go one step outside without I fix your arm." Caroline added a soft Please, and that changed his mind about his priorities right quick.

Fernanda insisted on removing his shirt and washing his flesh wound before she would set foot outside the hotel room door. Caroline, he noticed, turned away the instant his chest was bared.

"Ladies," Hawk said as Fernanda bandaged his arm, "I hear fiddle music. Seems like there's some kind of fandango going on here tonight. How about I buy us all a steak dinner to take some of the sting out of the last ten hours?"

Caroline's stomach was rumbling so loud it embarrassed her. She brushed the dust off her bombazine travel suit and followed Fernanda down to the dining room. Apparently the party was in the adjoining ballroom because the restaurant was deserted except for an overweight man at the table nearest the entrance.

He looked up, then stood and surveyed them with hard blue eyes. To her astonishment, as they approached Hawk touched his hat brim with two fingers. "Will," he said quietly.

"Hawk," the large man replied. "Haven't seen you in a while."

"Don't get this far north very often."

"Yeah, I know."

Hawk guided Fernanda and Caroline past the man to a table at the back of the room.

"What brings you this time?" the man queried.

Hawk seated them at a round cloth-covered table, then removed his hat and folded himself into the third chair. "Nursemaiding," he said blandly.

Fernanda laughed, but Caroline's hands turned into fists in her lap.

"Yeah?" The man called Will gave them a slow once-over with his pale eyes. "That what you call it? Looks more like—"

"Button it, Paine," Hawk cut in.

The man's blond eyebrows rose. "You gonna introduce me?"

"Nope. What are you doing here, anyway?"

Paine settled back onto his chair. "Big wingding in town tonight. Mayor's daughter got herself engaged. I'm here to keep the peace."

Caroline stared at Hawk. "This man, Will, is a lawman?" she whispered. "Why, he doesn't even wear a badge."

Hawk drew her attention away by tapping his

forefinger on the menu. "Order me a steak," he said. "I'll be right back." He stood and crossed the room to Will's table, spun the chair backward and straddled it. The two men bent their heads together and spoke so quietly she couldn't understand a word.

When Hawk returned, his eyes were narrowed and his mouth was pressed into an unsmiling line. Fernanda patted his hand. "You fight with your friend, *señor*?"

"He's not exactly a friend," Hawk growled. "We rode together some years back."

"You do not like each other no more?"

"Oh, we like each other well enough. It's just that he's too damn busy with the mayor's daughter to escort you on to Idaho."

"And you wish he would," Caroline said quietly. "Because you do not want to." She could not blame him one bit. He'd risked his life, endured a bullet wound and was obviously disgusted with her cause. And her. But even so, she wanted…

What did she want?

She wanted to feel safe, protected by this

man. She was a little in awe of him, even a little fluttery deep inside when he looked at her. She liked being near him.

But of course he would want to return to his home in Smoke River.

"Are you married?" she blurted out.

He settled his green eyes on hers and in their depths she saw an unnerving combination of pain and hunger. "Was once. She was killed." Then the curtain dropped over his expression, shutting her out.

For the second time in the last twenty-four hours, Caroline could think of nothing to say.

"Got any more questions?" He signaled for the waitress.

She shook her head, feeling her color rise.

"Good, because I've got a couple. First, what the hell are you doing this speech stuff for?"

"I told you, I am campaigning to give women the vote."

"No, I mean *why* are you doing this? Why are you risking your life to make speeches?"

Caroline exchanged a look with Fernanda. She could evade the question. Prevaricate, or just plain lie. Or she could tell him the truth. Before she could open her mouth, he spoke again.

"I know your father bullied your mother," he said. "You explained that in your speech at the church in Gillette Springs. Is that it?"

"N-no. At least that's not all of it." Under the high collar of her blue dress she felt her throat close.

The waitress approached, pad and pencil in her hand. Rivera ordered steak, rare. Fernanda ordered the same. Caroline couldn't make a sound.

"You hungry?" he murmured.

She nodded, her cheeks burning.

"She'll have a steak, medium rare. And some...tea?"

Again she nodded. Fernanda touched her hand. "*Hija*, you do not need to answer the questions. Does she, *señor*?"

Hawk shook his head. "No, she doesn't. Everyone's got a right to a private life."

"Even you, *señor*," Fernanda pointed out with a twinkle in her black eyes. "But you will tell us why you look angry when you talk to Mr. Paine?"

Hawk blew out a long breath. "I want—wanted—Will Paine to take you on to Idaho."

"And he cannot," Fernanda pressed. "So you are angry with him. And that is because?"

Hawk couldn't begin to answer that question. Because he wanted to go back to Smoke River, back to peace and quiet in the little town he'd sought out to heal the festering wound in his soul. Because he didn't want to be responsible ever again for someone that meant anything to him.

Aw, hell, why not admit it. Because he didn't want to see Caroline get hurt.

Supper didn't improve his outlook. The steak was fork-tender, the apple pie was succulent and the coffee hot and strong, but still everything seemed wrong. Out of kilter. He'd lugged his saddlebag with him into the hotel, but inside he had only one clean shirt and a pair of drawers, plus three boxes of cartridges and a hunk of jerky. If he was gonna spend another night sleeping in the same room with

Caroline and Fernanda, he needed a bath and some clean clothes.

They hadn't objected to sharing the room with him last night, but tonight he was dirtier and sweatier and so tired that rolling himself up in a quilt and sleeping on the floor in front of the door held less appeal, especially when a nice soft bed sat just six feet away.

Both Caroline and Fernanda had been quiet throughout the meal, Fernanda absorbed in her steak and Caroline because she couldn't seem to relax. She fiddled with her knife, her fork, her teacup, even the buttons on her blue dress. Maybe she was uneasy about the sleeping arrangements? She hadn't seemed to mind his presence last night in Gillette Springs, but she'd just had the spit scared out of her by that note.

Or maybe she was scared about tomorrow. She was making another damned speech at ten o'clock, this time at some ladies' auxiliary hall down the street from the hotel. He drank the last of his coffee and studied her face.

Hell, she looked nervous already. At the church the other night she'd looked cool and composed right up until she got that note. Now she looked like she had a case of stage fright so bad it would freeze up Sarah Bernhardt.

He wanted to know why. Why did she persist when she was clearly frightened? He wanted to know a lot of things. Women were so unexplainable it was a wonder a man ever got close enough to marry one.

The sound of guitars and banjos and a violin drifted from the ballroom. Then a low thump sounded, and Will Paine got up and went off to "keep order," Hawk guessed. When he heard another thump and then a pistol shot, his first impulse was to back the man up. But his second impulse was stronger: sit tight and make sure no one got within striking distance of the two females under his care.

Another pistol shot went off, and Caroline jumped and hissed air into her lungs. He looked at her face and swore under his breath. She'd turned another pasty shade of white.

"You about ready to turn in?"

She was out of her chair before he could set his coffee cup down. He tossed bills onto the table, tore after her and caught her at the doorway.

"Wait up," he ordered. "You don't go anywhere without me, remember?"

Caroline halted. "Oh. I was in such a hurry I forgot." Well, no, she hadn't forgotten, exactly. It was just that she could not sit still when a gunshot sounded, even with Hawk Rivera at her elbow.

Oh, Mama, were you this frightened? How strong and calm you always seemed.

And her mother had not had Hawk Rivera protecting her. She wondered if it would have made a difference.

He took her arm and kept her close at his side, so close she could feel his chest move in and out with each breath. For one insane moment she wanted to turn into his arms and press her face to his chest, listen to his heartbeat. While her own pulse was ragged, she was sure his would be strong and steady.

She shook herself out of the thought and concentrated on putting one foot in front of the other. The dance music grew fainter as they climbed the three sets of stairs up to the hotel room. When he unlocked the door, Fernanda marched inside, spun, and pointed to Hawk's dusty leather saddlebag in the corner.

"You have clean clothes?"

"Yeah. What I've got on me could stand up all by themselves."

"Then take them off. I go find a basin to wash."

"No." He blocked the doorway. "I'll have a bathtub sent up, one for you and Caroline, and another for me and my clothes."

"Ah, no, *señor.* Is not proper."

"Proper! Hell, I haven't let either one of you out of my sight for two solid days, what's 'proper' got to do with it?"

Fernanda set her hands on her hips. "Is not proper for a man to wash his own clothes."

"*Señora*, I've been a bachelor for twelve years. That's a lot of laundry."

"And no woman, eh?"

"No woman."

Caroline ducked her head to hide the smile she couldn't hold back. No woman. *No woman.*

Oh, for pity's sake what was wrong with her? She didn't care if he had a dozen women, which he no doubt had, looking the way he did. A more ruggedly handsome man she had never seen.

And a more foolish girl you have never met. She and Hawk Rivera were as different as horses and cheese.

"Go, then," Fernanda said to him. "Tell them to bring soap, also. Pretty smelling."

Hawk groaned, and Caroline tamped down an unexpected spurt of laughter.

Four giggling Mexican hotel maids hauled in the two bathtubs and filled them with buckets of steaming water. Hawk discreetly withdrew to the hallway, where he walked up and down, listening to the feminine squeals and laughter floating out of the room. God, a woman sure liked to splash around in a tub of water.

He tried to keep his mind on the pattern in the carpet under his feet, on the rose-flowered wallpaper covering the walls, on anything but Caroline's slim body naked in a bathtub.

Didn't work. When Fernanda summoned him with a whispered "Your turn, *señor*," he was hard as Texas granite.

Inside, Caroline was drying her long hair with a towel while Fernanda soused some garments up and down in their used bathwater. Small garments. She had strung up a makeshift clothesline with a length of grocery string, and when she started hanging up the wet clothes he noted what they were: lacy camisoles. Pantalets with ruffles. Two petticoats and a corset cover with an embroidered rosebud in the center. His hard-on got a lot harder.

"Now you, *señor*."

He dropped his gun and holster on the floor where he stood and started to undo his belt, then paused. "I allowed you ladies some privacy—how about you doing the same for me?"

Caroline sent him a quick glance, but Fernanda grinned at him. "You do not mind if we are wander outside alone?"

"Forget it," he amended. "You don't go anywhere unless I can see you."

The Mexican woman blinked. "Even to the necessary? Is just down the hallway, *señor*."

"I'll go with you. Either that or use the chamber pot."

Caroline turned scarlet.

He unhooked his belt buckle. "Turn around, both of you."

They about-faced so fast he'd swear they had military training. But not military discipline. The minute he splashed into the tub, Fernanda pounced on his clothes and tossed them into the other tub. Caroline kept her back to him.

He slid down to rest his neck on the metal edge and closed his eyes. A bathtub was one of the seven wonders of the world.

He massaged his wounded arm, assuring himself it was just a flesh wound and that it wasn't getting infected, then slapped a soapy cloth all over his body. Lilac scent bloomed under his nose. Ladies' scent. Caroline's scent. God. He hoped neither of them could see his privates through the bathwater.

He rinsed off and stood up to find Fernanda

pinning his laundered shirt and drawers to the clothesline. He toweled himself dry, suddenly wondering what Caroline would think of his scarred body, the chest wound he'd taken two years ago, the parallel knife slashes across his midriff.

Her voice jarred him. "Are you decent?" she asked. "May I turn around now?"

"Not yet." He walked to his saddlebag and pulled out his remaining clean shirt and a pair of drawers. He'd just finished buttoning his trousers when Fernanda gave a little yip.

"*Ay de mi, señor.* You are *muy* cut up!"

Before he could get his shirt closed, Caroline spun around, a hairbrush clutched in her hand. "Have you been wounded before? In the War?"

"One war," he gritted. "And one private fight." He wished she hadn't seen his bare chest. It was easier to pretend it had never happened when the scars were hidden under a layer of clothing.

But she had seen, and the look on her face

stopped his breath. "Is—is that what a gunshot wound in the chest looks like?"

"Somewhat. This one's mostly healed over."

"My God. Oh, my God." She dropped the hairbrush and hid her face in her hands.

"What?" He reached her in two steps. "What is wrong?"

"Tell him, *mi corazón*. Tell him."

"I can't," she said, her voice muffled.

"Tell me what?" Hawk demanded. He grasped her shoulders and gave her a little shake. "Tell me what?"

Silence. He could hear her uneven breathing, feel her body tremble under his hands. And, goddamn, he could smell the lilac scent of her hair.

"*Señor*, do not ask her this thing. She is not yet ready to speak of it."

Hawk felt like a coal shovel had been whacked over his skull. He wanted to pick her up and hold her in his arms and never let go.

She broke away and perched on the edge of the bed. Very slowly she lifted her face and looked at him. "I am speaking tomorrow. I am trying very hard to not be afraid."

"The hell you are," he snapped out.

"Speaking? Or afraid?" Her voice was calm, but her widened deep blue eyes were frightened.

"Don't do it," he said. "Don't give your damn speech."

"I must." And then she sent him that little smile that made mincemeat of his insides. "And it is not a 'damn speech.'"

He couldn't stand looking at her one more minute. Instead he went over to the window and peered down at the street below. Dressmaker. Sheriff's office. Mercantile. Red Rooster Saloon. Another saloon. He wondered where Overby was. Was Oakridge his final destination?

He didn't like the man. Didn't trust him. For all Hawk knew, Overby could have tipped off someone when they stopped for the meal at the Tumbleweed way station. The thought ate at him.

Finally he grabbed the quilt off the other

bed, checked his revolver and laid the rifle down next to the far wall. Then he rolled himself up in the soft blanket, squashed his saddlebag under his head for a pillow and tried to sleep.

With his eyes closed, every sound in the room inflamed his imagination: Fernanda's humming, her shoes hitting the floor, the sound of the bedsprings when she settled down. But there wasn't a sound from Caroline.

Had she undressed? Slipped into the bed by the window? Or was she still sitting on the edge of the mattress, drying her hair? He cracked one lid open.

Her back was toward him, her arm lifting and dropping, slowly pulling the hairbrush through the thick, dark waves. At the end of each stroke she smoothed her other hand down the entire length, and then repeated the motion. Watching her was unsettling. Arousing. He ground his teeth and shut his eyes.

Fernanda's humming lapsed into light snores, and still Caroline made no sound— no petticoat rustles, no shoe dropping onto the carpet. What the hell was she doing, just sitting there staring out the window?

The glass lamp cover scraped and a breath puffed out the light. And then nothing.

"Caroline?" He spoke quietly so Fernanda wouldn't wake up.

"Yes?"

"Are you all right?"

There was a long, long pause before she answered. "I will be. It is always hard at night when I start to remember…things."

Hawk sat up. "What things?"

She didn't answer. After a while he heard the swish of bedcovers.

It took a long time before her breathing evened out and deepened into sleep. Hawk lay back down, puzzling over the hollow feeling that bloomed deep in his gut.

Chapter Nine

I am worry for my lady. She is good soldier, but she is a woman, not a soldier. She think she must do this thing, and she is right maybe, but the risk, it is great.

This man, *Señor* Hawk, try to protect her. I pray to the Virgin every night he will do so, but my lady she is stubborn like bull, even though she look like delicate butterfly.

Each day I grow older by ten years. When we reach the end of this journey, my hair it will be white like albino goat. *Ay de mi*, what a hard thing this is to watch.

Caroline inspected her face in the mirror mounted in the back room of the Oakridge

Ladies Auxiliary hall. And scrunched her eyes shut. She looked ravaged. Dark circles spread like bruises under her eyes and her skin was so devoid of color she looked like a ghost.

Despite Hawk's advice, she had pinned her hair in the usual bun at her neck. Her concession to looking "softer," as he had suggested, was the yellow calico skirt and ruffled shirt-waist she now wore. There shouldn't be many men at an auxiliary meeting, so it wouldn't really matter how she dressed.

She wiped her damp palms down the sides of her skirt, straightened her shoulders and stepped out into the hall. Fernanda planted her plump form at her side. Sheriff Will Paine stood in the back, collecting the weapons from the few men as they entered.

Hawk stepped in front of her and signaled that all was clear. He was carrying his rifle, she noticed. She knew she would be protected, but fear lay sour in the pit of her stomach and she had to keep swallowing to forestall the nausea that threatened.

Mama must have had nerves like iron rail-

road spikes. She sucked in air, moved into the hall and faced her audience.

A sea of placards waved. WOMEN STAND UNITED. VOTING RIGHTS ARE SACRED. DOWN WITH MALE DOMINATION.

Oh, mercy. Men did not like to be accused of bullying.

She made her way toward the raised platform amid a spattering of applause, but when she saw there was no lectern to position herself behind, her step faltered. She would be dreadfully exposed. She glanced at Hawk, saw his gaze scan the area where she would stand, and after a moment he nodded at her.

She walked forward, ascended the single step and moved to the center of the platform. Then she turned and smiled at the crowd.

Hawk placed himself two steps behind her and slightly to the left, keeping his lifted rifle visible this time to get the message across: harm her and you won't live to tell about it.

He studied the men in the audience, caught Will Paine's eye and raised his eyebrows. Will gave him a lazy thumbs-up. Hawk prayed the sheriff had confiscated all the weapons without missing any.

Caroline began to speak, keeping her voice calm and even, without even a tremor to reveal how frightened she was. Hawk knew she was terrified because the hands she clasped behind her back were shaking like aspen leaves in a breeze.

"Ladies and gentlemen, thank you for coming to hear my views on why women should be allowed to vote." She paused and swallowed.

"We're waitin', honey," a man called from the back. "We ain't convinced, are we, gents?"

A chorus of No's rolled over her.

"Well, then, gentlemen, I shall try to convince you. Did you know that when a woman marries, all her property, money in her bank account, a house, farmland, even the clothes on her back no longer belong to her? What she once owned now belongs to her husband."

"Huh! That why you ain't hitched, lady?"

Hawk winced. Some men sure liked hitting below the belt. But he hadn't realized that a man owned a woman's property no matter what.

"No, it is not," she countered. "My marital preference is not at issue here. The issue here is fairness. The truth is, gentlemen, that women are not a race to be subjected, to be turned into slaves. A women is your equal."

"Not hardly!" someone yelled.

"Why not?" a woman screamed in answer. "I'm just as smart as you!"

Another woman in a pink gingham dress shot to her feet. "I work just as hard as any man. Harder, if you count havin' babies."

"And," Caroline interjected, "that is exactly the point. Now, I must compliment the state of Oregon, which has had the foresight to allow a woman to homestead on her own. Six hundred forty acres can be claimed by a single woman. But let us say she falls in love with her neighbor, also a homesteader, and they want to get married. Did you know that the minute she says 'I do' her homestead no longer belongs to her? It now belongs to her husband. If he wants to, he can sell it out from under her and he will not owe her one red cent."

"That ain't true," a man bellowed.

"Oh, yes it is true," Caroline returned. "Ask any judge in any county in this state."

Hawk blinked. If that was true, it was damned unfair. All at once he wondered if his mother would have wanted the vote.

A burly man stood up and stuffed his thumbs in his overall straps. "Iff'n you ladies get the vote, first thing you'll do is start outlawin' things like gambling and, well, fancy ladies."

"And," another farmer shouted, "just so's you all know, ma'am, men hafta have some kind of, um, release every so often."

Caroline kept her voice level. "Sir, I do not think giving women the vote would prevent any man from, well, enjoying his, uh, release."

"Sure it would, little lady. Ya see, some women don't much like sex."

Caroline blushed to her hairline. "Yes, I—I do see."

Hawk bit the inside of his cheek. He'd bet she didn't even have a glimmer. Didn't even think about it. Then he had to wonder why she *didn't* think about it. Men certainly gave her an appreciative once-over wherever she went. He'd seen it every time she appeared in public. So wasn't she interested in the male of the species?

Next time he got her alone, he'd ask her.

He chomped down on the other side of his cheek. *Like hell he would.*

He shoved her speech-making to the back of his mind and began to plan how to get her safely onto the train after her speech. The eastbound Union Pacific to Boise left at one o'clock, right after she finished up her talk. Anything could happen between here and the train station.

Already the crowd was getting raucous, and questions and insults began to fly. Hawk studied the body language of the men, trying to anticipate where trouble might start, when some infuriated rancher would do something he'd regret.

As Caroline's hour-long speech wound down, he couldn't help frowning. The men in her audience were vocal, quarrelsome, even accusing, but no gunplay had started, and no threatening notes had been delivered by some innocent-looking kid.

What was he *not* seeing?

He envisioned the three long blocks from here to the train station, blocks she'd have to negotiate on foot. Even though she'd be flanked by Fernanda and himself, she would be out in the open and so vulnerable it made his flesh crawl. Part of him wanted to wrap her up inside his skin and keep her safe. Another part of him wanted—what?

He wanted this whole damn exercise in free speech to be over. He wanted to barge into a saloon and gulp down more than a few slugs of whiskey instead of worrying that someone was going to shoot her or kidnap her or worse. He wouldn't relax until the train to Idaho started rolling down the tracks. Good thing he'd left his deputy, Sandy, back at Smoke River. Sandy could handle whatever might come up while he was away.

She finished her talk, and with a gracious smile accepted the applause, right along with loud boos from the men. Then she turned to him, a look of both relief and triumph on her face. His nerves felt strung up tight as new barbed wire, but he tried to smile at her anyway.

All the way to the train he kept her close, discreetly resting his arm around her slim waist while Fernanda walked on her other side, one hand in her skirt pocket where she carried her pistol. He wondered if Caroline was doing the same.

Nope. Her arms swung at her sides. If she still had the weapon he'd bought for her, it sure wasn't in her pocket.

They crossed the last street before the train station. One more block. "Where's your pistol?" he asked.

"In my trunk."

He stopped short. "Dammit, you're supposed to keep it within reach."

She looked up at him with that half smile. "*You* are within reach, Mr. Rivera. I do not need the pistol."

He yanked her around to face him. "That kind of thinking could get you killed, you know that? I can't always be here, dogging your every goddamn move, Caroline. Makes me want to—"

He broke off. Made him want to tuck her into his pocket or haul her up and load her over his shoulder. God, she could make a man sweat nails.

Caroline recoiled at the anger in his voice. The steely look in those green eyes of his sent a shudder up her backbone, and all at once she became aware of something she had not wanted to think about. Hawk *was* with her; but he most certainly did not want to be.

"What happens in Boise?" he asked suddenly.

"I make another speech."

"What happens *after* Boise?"

"From Boise, we plan to travel north, to Washington Territory. But I am sure—"

"I'm not," he gritted. "I want you to skip Washington. Stop putting yourself in the line of fire and go home to Boston." He jerked her forward and matched his long stride to her shorter steps.

"I cannot do that," she said, her voice quiet.

"You mean you *won't* do that, not that you 'can't.'"

"You could never understand. Never. All right then, I won't. That does not mean you have to…"

Beside her Fernanda hissed a warning. "*Mi corazón*, do not toss away a man's pride."

"His pride?" she murmured so he would not hear. "What has his pride to do with it?"

"Ah, you are more pigheaded than even your *madre*. And more ignorant. Even I, Fernanda Elena Maria Sobrano, know that a man's pride is most important thing not to make little."

"Damn straight," Hawk intoned.

"*Señor*, you are not to listen!"

"*Señora*, just try and stop me."

"Oh, for pity's sake," Caroline blurted out. "Hush up, both of you."

They reached the train station enveloped in an awkward silence. Hawk peeled some bills out of his vest pocket and sent Fernanda in to purchase the tickets. The minute she was out of earshot, he maneuvered Caroline over to a wall, turned her so her back pressed against the boards, and planted both elbows over her head.

"There's something we need to settle between us here and now," he said near her temple. His breath warmed her ear, sending an odd tremor through her.

"I'm not leaving you, Caroline. You can travel all over hell and gone, but I'm not letting you out of my sight."

She opened her mouth to respond but he cut her off. "I signed on to protect you and by God that's what I intend to do."

Again she opened her lips, but he placed his hand over her mouth. "So you just shut the hell up about what you want and do what I say."

She was so mad she could spit bullets. She hated being bossed around. She hated being frightened. She hated *him*. She clamped her lips together so he wouldn't see them tremble.

Fernanda returned, gave them both a raised eyebrow and stuffed the train tickets into Hawk's hand. "I hope you still want us, *señor*," she murmured. "Because I think my lady is *muy furioso*."

Hawk snorted. Oh, he wanted them all right. Fernanda was an admirable example of good sense and guts, and Caroline…

Caroline was strong and soft and beautiful and vulnerable and everything in between. Caroline MacFarlane was a whole helluva lot more than he'd bargained for. When they reached Boise, he'd lock them both into their hotel room and find the nearest saloon and get good and drunk.

The locomotive chuffed into the station and steamed to a stop. Hawk directed the porter to load the trunk, then manhandled both women into the passenger car and sat them down facing across from him. The engine started to roll forward.

Hawk let out a sigh of relief and watched the station glide past the window. Just as the train picked up speed, a tall figure in a derby hat sprinted out of the station house and launched himself onto the iron loading step.

Overby.

Chapter Ten

Hawk didn't sleep during the entire eight-hour trip across the dry, flat high Oregon desert into Idaho. He couldn't nod off and leave Caroline unprotected, and he couldn't go looking for Overby for the same reason. He couldn't shuck the feeling that something was about to happen. It reminded him of his Ranger days back in Texas, where he spent long days and hundreds of miles with his rifle primed and his nerves feeling like spiny cactus.

Next to Caroline, Fernanda dozed in the seat across from him. The younger woman kept tipping toward Fernanda but she righted herself at the last minute and jolted awake. Her skin looked gray with fatigue and her eyelids were shadowed. Finally he couldn't stand it one more minute, and when she slumped to the left, he stood, slid his arm under her knees and lifted her over to his side. She didn't even wake up, just gave a soft sigh and snuggled up against him.

He rested his hand on her shoulder until his arm went to sleep, then gritted his teeth and flexed his fingers to get the feeling back. The scent of her hair drove him half-crazy. He tried not to inhale, but it was a losing battle; her head fit just under his jaw and tendrils of dark curls were escaping the bun at her neck. The soft, sweet-smelling strands tickled his chin, teasing his body into arousal. She could sure do things to a man.

It was full dark when the train pulled into Boise. Hawk directed the porter to send the trunk to the nearest hotel, then lifted his hand from Caroline's shoulder and jiggled his boot against Fernanda's leather shoe.

"We are here, *si*?" the Mexican woman asked.

"We are here." He rose and offered his hand to Caroline. "Come on."

After a slight hesitation, her fingers twined into his; he pulled her upright and steadied her on her feet. Fernanda followed him to the iron debarking step, but before he stepped off the train he released his grip on Caroline's arm and scanned the platform for any sign of Overby.

He also made sure he could reach his revolver in a hurry.

Behind him Fernanda said something in Spanish, but all he caught was the word *padre*. That made no sense until he spied the Catholic Church across the street.

"I wish to go and light candle, *señor*." She tipped her head at the carved statue of Jesus over the wooden doorway. "I find you at hotel, later." She headed for the church entrance and Hawk turned to Caroline.

"You hungry?"

"You ask me that a lot," she said, her voice still drowsy.

"Must be because I get that way a lot."

She laughed softly. "Oh. Yes, I am hungry, now that I think of it."

He guided her into the hotel, stopped at the desk to register and give instructions about the trunk, then veered into the adjoining dining room. The dimly lit place was almost empty except for one table, occupied by a young, schoolteacherish man with spectacles. Not Overby.

When they were seated, Hawk made sure he could see the restaurant entrance from his chair and that the schoolteacher wasn't in his line of fire.

Caroline watched Rivera capture the attention of the lone waitress and order coffee and some tea for her. He looked a little ill at ease, and then she realized why. This was the first time they had been alone together, without Fernanda. Though why a man like Hawk would find that awkward she could not imagine. Hawk Rivera would certainly be used to the company of women; those eyes of his, the angular, tanned features, his dark mustache curving over his lips all told her in no uncertain terms that women would find him attractive. No doubt he was attracted to them, as well.

But perhaps not to her. She studied her cup of tea when it came, ordered a light supper of potato soup and some bread and found herself inexplicably tongue-tied. Evidently he, too, could think of nothing to say because the silence between them stretched until she thought she would scream.

"You're not a churchgoer, I guess," he said at last.

"What? Oh, you mean Fernanda and her candles. No, I am not. I stopped attending church after I…after I grew up."

His green eyes questioned, but she closed her lips decisively. The waitress brought her soup, along with his steak and fried potatoes, and then dawdled over the plates admiring Rivera's good looks. Then with a quick, envious glance at Caroline, the young woman disappeared into the kitchen and they were alone again.

More silence. She noticed Hawk wasn't cutting into his steak. In fact he wasn't doing anything except staring at her.

"What is it? Is my hair straggling out of my bun?"

"Yeah, some. Don't worry about it, looks kinda… Don't worry about it."

She touched the nape of her neck. "Kind of what?"

"Kinda pretty."

"Pretty?" She felt the word all the way down to her toes. "As in…woman-pretty?" Oh, she could have cut off her tongue when she heard what she'd said.

He didn't answer, just dropped his gaze and picked up his knife and fork. "Tell me something," he said, slicing into the meat. "I know you want women to get the vote and be treated as equals."

"Yes. Do you not think men and woman are equals?"

"Never thought about it much."

She lifted her teacup. "Well, think about it now, why don't you?"

He looked straight into her eyes. "Guess I've always felt women were plenty equal, seein' as they have us men over a barrel."

"Oh? How is that, exactly? Over a barrel, I mean."

He drew in a long breath, looked away, and then looked back at her. "A man…men need women."

"You mean they need women to *do* for them, cook and wash and clean and bear his children?"

"Not so much, no. A man can do all those things for himself. He can cook and wash and all the rest, except for having babies. I mean that a man, uh, men *like* women. Like having them around. Like looking at them. Touching them."

She swallowed. "I see."

"Don't think you do, really," he said. "See, a man doesn't feel exactly equal to a woman because he never knows what she's thinking. Or feeling."

"And you think a woman always knows what a man is thinking, is that it? Let me tell you something, Mr. Rivera, I haven't had the foggiest inkling about what *you're* thinking or feeling since we met. So I don't feel 'equal'—I feel…off balance." She was going to say *overwhelmed* but thought better of it.

He surprised her by grinning so broadly his whole countenance lit up. The man had simply beautiful teeth—straight and white against his tanned skin. Her heart gave a little skip.

And then suddenly his face sobered and he leaned toward her. "There's more to it, though, isn't there? Tell me the real reason you're traveling around making all these speeches."

Caroline jerked and thick soup slopped out of her spoon.

"Tell me why," he pursued.

She tried to breathe normally, but her pulse began to race. "My mother and I…" She had to stop and start over. "My mother met Elizabeth Cady Stanton, the suffragette, when I was twelve. Mama and I had moved to Philadelphia because… Anyway, Mrs. Stanton took us in. Later Mama began to travel and speak out for women. For their rights."

She found herself tearing a slice of bread into tiny pieces.

"How old were you then?"

"I was just seventeen."

His dark eyebrows rose. "How old are you now?"

She hesitated. Oh, what did it matter? He didn't care if she was a hundred and two. "I am twenty-five."

He regarded her in silence for a long minute. "You look much younger. At least you do when you're not exhausted."

She bit back an unladylike snort of laughter. "I hold no illusions about my age, Mr. Rivera. I am a spinster. 'On the shelf' we would say back in Boston."

To her surprise, he chuckled. "Might say that in Boston, but a man sure wouldn't say that out here in the West." He forked a bite of steak past his lips and chewed while she stared at him.

He swallowed, still holding her gaze. "What happened to your mother?"

"Mama got sick. By the time we reached Texas, she was coughing up blood and…" Her throat closed.

"And?" he prompted. Instead of looking at

her, he deliberately addressed the potatoes on his plate.

"That is when I hired Fernanda. The priest at the mission brought her to me."

"Padre Ralph," he murmured.

"Why, yes. Fernanda helped me nurse Mama until she died."

"And then you…?" He left the question hanging.

"Mama made me p-promise to carry on traveling and speaking out for women. Fernanda left Texas to accompany me."

He said nothing for so long she wondered if he regretted his probing.

"I know Father Ralph. Or rather I knew him. I come from Texas, from Butte City, where Father Ralph's mission is. You knew that, didn't you?"

"Yes. Fernanda told me. She confessed how she found you. How she threatened you, most likely."

"She didn't have to threaten very hard. Fernanda knew my mother."

Caroline blinked. "*That* she did *not* tell me. Your mother was…at the mission, perhaps?"

He laid down his fork. "No. My mother was Marguerite Anderson. She and my father owned most of Butte City."

"Oh?"

"She was English. My father was Luis de Avalos-Rivera. Don Luis. Big ranches. Money."

"You are educated, are you not?"

"Some. My mother hired tutors. My father hired vaqueros. Ranch hands."

"Is that why you ride so well? And shoot a gun with accuracy? Why you were a Texas Ranger?"

"Partly. I didn't join the Rangers until after my mother died. She was killed, along with my wife."

Caroline's hand flew to her mouth and a spoonful of soup splashed onto the tablecloth. "Oh, my God," she breathed.

Hawk reached out and tugged her hand back to her soupspoon. "Eat. The dead are dead."

She gazed at him with stricken eyes, the

blue so dark it shaded into purple. He'd thought it wouldn't affect him to tell her, but it did. In a funny way he felt lighter, as if the hard knot he'd carried inside his gut all these years had loosened just a bit.

"Eat," he repeated. "Your next speech is tomorrow, isn't it?"

She nodded and began tearing apart another slice of bread. He rescued it before the crumbs covered the tablecloth.

"What time?"

"Noon."

"Where?"

"In the town square."

His knife clattered onto his plate. "What? You mean outside?"

"Yes."

He sent her a look that would curdle milk. "What idiot arranged that?"

"Mama had arranged it. I promised—"

"I don't care what you promised," he grated. "Change it."

"I cannot. The women's league in Boise

made all the arrangements. It is too late to change them now."

"Caroline, it's dangerous."

"I— But you will be there."

"Dammit, I'm not God."

Fernanda appeared at his elbow. "Who is not God, *señor*?"

Hawk groaned. He hadn't even seen her enter the room.

"Fernanda," Caroline explained, "Hawk is concerned about my speech tomorrow."

The Mexican woman plopped her bulk into the empty seat and snatched up a slice of Caroline's bread. "So he should be."

Hawk summoned the waitress with a gesture. "Order some supper, *señora*. All that praying must have given you an appetite."

Before Fernanda finished speaking to the waitress, Hawk pushed back his chair. "Come on. We're going upstairs."

Caroline's gaze darted to Fernanda. "I cannot leave her alone."

"*Si, mi corazón*, you can. Go. You look tired, like…" She purposely slumped her shoulders to demonstrate. "Like warm-over tamale. And I am hungry."

Hawk gripped her elbow so hard she gave a little whimper. "Sorry," he muttered. "Fernanda's right. You do look like a warmed-over tamale."

Chapter Eleven

Hawk unlocked the door to their hotel room and pushed Caroline inside. Neither had spoken a word since leaving Fernanda in the dining room, devouring a plate of chili and beans, but he was way past being conversational.

Moonlight slanted through the single window. He lit the lamp, hauled the trunk over to her side of the room and stood, wondering why he was so uneasy. After all, it wasn't the first time he'd been alone in a hotel room with a woman.

But he'd never been alone with Caroline. He hated it.

Correction, he liked it.

Too much.

He stepped to the window and stood looking out on the busy street below. His heartbeat wasn't the least bit normal and his chest felt tight. He shouldn't have said so much about himself at supper. He felt like he'd opened a crack into a dark part of himself.

Worst of all, his jeans were suddenly too tight and it didn't take a genius to figure out why. He'd been hard since he'd spent the last hour watching Caroline's lips open and close around that damned soupspoon.

He'd be all right as soon as Fernanda returned and he could focus on something other than the tense, hungry feeling eating him up from the inside. Better get his mind off it.

He swung around and stopped short. Caroline was facing away from him, her hands raised, unpinning the twisted bun gathered at the back of her neck. Something zinged up his spine and his control snapped.

He moved behind her, lifted away the remaining pins and dropped them one by one onto the carpeted floor. Then very slowly he threaded his fingers through her thick hair.

Her breath hissed in, and then her head tipped back against his hands.

"Caroline." He scarcely recognized his own voice. Scarcely aware of what he was doing, he deliberately turned her to face him, bent his head and caught her mouth under his.

He didn't know how long he moved over her lips, but he did know he never wanted to stop. She was sweet beyond belief, and soft. And female. So damn female he ached all over.

And then her open hand cracked across his cheek so hard the skin burned.

"Don't you ever, ever do that again!" she shouted.

He could see her body shaking; the ruffles down the front of her shirtwaist trembled. He stared at her. Her eyes blazed into his and without thinking he reached for her arm.

"Stay away," she warned. "Just stay away from me."

What the—? He stepped back but he couldn't stop looking at her. He'd never misjudged a woman this badly since he was a green boy of fourteen.

At that moment, the unlocked door opened with a bang and Fernanda bustled in. Instantly she halted and peered from Caroline to him and back again, one eyebrow quirked. She said nothing, but Hawk knew the Mexican woman was no fool. She'd sensed the tension in the air and had wisely decided not to ask questions.

God bless her.

Caroline turned away from Fernanda's assessing gaze and Hawk strode out the door she had left open. "I'll be in the bar," he announced.

Caroline stared after him. Oh, how she wished she liked the taste of spirits. She could surely use a big, big glass of something to settle her jangled nerves. Or maybe deaden her mind.

She paced around and around the small room while Fernanda flitted from the trunk to the tall wardrobe on the far wall to the ceramic washbasin on the bureau, saying nothing. She could send her Mexican companion down to the bar for a flask of whiskey, but she knew Fernanda would never leave her alone, especially since Hawk was not here.

She pressed the heels of her hands into her eyes hard enough to hurt. *Heaven help her, she was so tired of this.* Tired of being afraid. Tired of the worry about everything, about herself, about what the rest of her life was beginning to look like. She was even tired of her speaking circuit, the one she had promised Mama she would continue.

Mostly, she realized, she was tired of not feeling natural, like other women felt when a man approached them. Perhaps she never would. The instant Hawk's mouth had touched hers she felt the old panic start. God in heaven, would she never be free?

Her right hand still tingled where she had struck him. Using her left, she unbuttoned the shirtwaist and skirt and let them drop to the floor along with her petticoats. Then she stumbled over to the bed nearest the window and crawled between the sheets, still wearing her camisole and underdrawers.

Fernanda picked up the garments, shook

out the wrinkles, hung them up and clicked the wardrobe door shut. Shaking her head, she surveyed the unmoving lump under Caroline's blanket-covered bed and worked to suppress the smile spreading across her face.

Hours later, *Señor* Hawk returned. Fernanda lay very still in her narrow bed, listening as he shucked his shirt and jeans and boots and rolled himself up in the quilt she had left for him. And then she smiled again. He was a good man.

God is good.

Chapter Twelve

Is not good what is happen now. Nobody
happy. Nobody laugh. The priest, he was
right, the world full of things we do not
understand.

But this I do understand. My lady she
is troubled in her heart. She is not a happy
woman. She not thinking clear, as God
intends. She is like her *madre*, all the time
watching and with the frown. All the time
waiting.

I hear her at night. She not know that I
listen, but I hear her dream bad things. I
hear her cry out, and then I hear her weep.

I think this will not end good, like I
had hope.

Hawk stretched his long frame out on the floor, positioning himself across the doorway as he had for the past four nights. Or was it five? It didn't matter. It wasn't going to end anytime soon.

He'd be damned if he'd give up now. He'd given his word to protect Caroline and he'd never yet gone back on a promise. And if he was honest with himself, it was more than just a promise; he couldn't stand the thought of anything happening to her.

He let out the breath he'd been holding. At the bar, he'd downed enough whiskey to drown a barrelful of pain, but it hadn't helped. It wasn't Caroline's slap across his face that hurt, it was knowing that she didn't want him. That she'd never want him, even if he was the last man in Idaho or Washington or wherever she was going.

But the worst part was something he hadn't counted on; she didn't want him, but by God, he wanted her.

He swallowed back a whiskey-laced bit of moisture and stifled a groan. What sane man would want a prickly, set-in-her-ways, stub-born suffragette lady in his bed?

He groaned again, this time out loud. He did. Hell's bells, he guessed he wasn't as sane as he'd thought.

For a long time he listened to Fernanda's and Caroline's steady breathing in the dark and tried not to follow where his thoughts wanted to take him. He had just closed his own eyes when he heard an odd sound. Not a thump, ex-actly, more like something heavy, like a glass, dropping onto the floor.

His neck hair prickled. It was a footstep, outside in the hall. Then another. The steps faded, then returned, then faded again.

His heart jumped into triple time. Some-one was walking up and down in the hallway. Maybe a man some woman had locked out of her room?

Maybe. The footsteps thudded past once more, and this time they stopped right out-side their door. Son of a blue-tailed fly. Very slowly, Hawk sat up and reached for his re-volver.

Overby?

He thumbed back the hammer, then rolled onto his knees and peered through the keyhole. Nothing, just a patch of patterned wallpaper on the opposite wall.

The footsteps returned, again stopping outside the door. Hawk squinted and now something dark appeared through the keyhole.

He was on his feet, yanking the door open, his revolver trained chest-high. A shadowed figure jerked away and bolted down the hall; then he heard footsteps pound down the stairs.

Hawk raced to the landing, but the staircase was empty. Far below he heard a door slam.

Damn. He padded quietly back into the room, shut the door and bolted it.

"Who was it?" Caroline's voice. She was sitting up in bed.

"You heard him? The footsteps?"

"Yes. I thought about getting my pistol from the trunk, but I was afraid I would wake Fernanda."

Hawk snorted. "Forget Fernanda. Whoever it is doesn't want Fernanda." He released the hammer on his revolver and stowed it under his pillow.

The bedclothes rustled. "Tomorrow…" She hesitated.

"Yeah? What about tomorrow? You change your mind?"

"N-no. But tomorrow I will keep my pistol in my skirt pocket, I promise."

Hawk lay down on top of the quilt, slipped the revolver under his hand and tried to stop his bad thoughts. "Go back to sleep, Caroline."

"I was not asleep."

"Don't tell me that, dammit. You need to sleep."

She said nothing for so long Hawk was certain she slept. Or he would have been certain except that he didn't hear any slow, rhythmic inhalations, and that meant she wasn't.

He lay in the quiet for a long time, listening.

When Caroline awoke, Hawk was gone. *Gone. Oh, dear God, what have I done?* She wished, oh, how she wished, she had not slapped him last night. She had wanted him to kiss her. If she were honest with herself she would have to admit she had been thinking about it for days. When she felt his hands in her hair her whole being had come alive, her blood thrumming through her veins like molten quicksilver.

But when his mouth had covered hers, she had panicked.

She squeezed her hands together so hard they hurt. She would never be normal, never be able to be close to a man, even one as trustworthy, as honorable, as Hawk Rivera. Now she had driven him away.

Fernanda eyed her as she climbed out of bed and stood at the chest of drawers, splashing cool water on her face. "*Hija*, you look like the devil has drag you around his boneyard."

"I am quite all right, Fernanda. Just tired. And I am a little worried about today."

Her companion planted her fists at her ample waist. "Is foolish thing you do today. *Señor* Hawk is right. You have the head of a pig."

Caroline gasped. "He said that? That I am pigheaded?"

"*Si*, pighead. Hawk leave before you wake to make sure—"

"He did?" Her spirits lifted. "You mean he is still here in town?"

Fernanda looked at her oddly. "*Sí*, in town. Of course here in town. What did you think?"

"I thought...well, I thought he might have left. Gone back to Oregon."

"Why he would do that?"

"Because I... Because he..."

Fernanda clucked her tongue. "Too many becauses. That man, he would not leave because you have bad words together."

"But I also—" She bit her tongue.

"Now hurry. You get ready for speaking. Hawk say to be ready when the church bell ring."

Caroline's hands shook as she donned the dark blue bombazine skirt and the matching high-necked top, not because of nerves, but because of the relief that washed through her. *Hawk had not left.*

The bell at the church across the street began to clang, and she quickly wound her hair into a twist at her neck and settled her hat on her head. She was just arranging the feather over one eye when someone tapped twice on the door.

Fernanda flew over to it, knocked smartly three times and undid the bolt.

Hawk strode in, his hat pulled low over his tanned features. When he looked up she saw the scowl. He looked furious, but she couldn't blame him. His eyes were hard as jade, and from the set of his mouth she doubted he would ever smile again.

"Ready?" His eyes raked over her. "I hate that hat," he muttered. "Makes you look sassy."

Fernanda's spurt of laughter caught him off guard. He cut his gaze to her. "Sassy isn't going to win women the vote. Sassy is going to make every woman in the audience jealous and every man wonder—" He bit off the rest of the thought.

"And good morning to you, too," Caroline said.

Fernanda threw up her hands. "Children, do not fight now! Do so later, when nerves have settle." Murmuring under her breath, she gathered up her black wool shawl and stomped out the door.

Caroline darted after her, but Hawk reached out and snagged her arm. "Stay behind me," he ordered.

She followed him down the staircase, and at the bottom he dropped back to walk next to her, holding his rifle in his free hand. Enticing food smells wafted from the dining room, and her stomach rumbled. Her steps slowed.

"Don't even think about it," he growled.

"But—"

"Later."

They walked in stony silence out the front entrance of the hotel and across the street to the grass-covered town park next to the church. It seemed like a thousand miles to the small wooden stage constructed in the shade of maple and ash trees dotting the area. With every step, Caroline tried to recall the opening words of her speech.

A good-sized crowd was gathered, some standing, some sitting on the grass. Around the perimeter stood five deputy sheriffs, badges winking in the dappled sunlight. A pile of gun belts and weapons mounded off to one side.

"How did those men know to—?"

"You think I went out before dawn to order bacon and eggs?"

"You went to the sheriff's office," she murmured.

"Damn straight."

"Hawk, thank you. Seeing them makes me feel much safer."

He didn't reply, just took her elbow as she ascended the single step. But instead of positioning herself behind the waiting lectern, she stepped to the front of the stage. Then, while Hawk watched in disbelief, she unpinned her hat and dropped it onto the wooden floor at her feet.

"Ladies and gentlemen," she began.

Hawk settled into position two steps behind her and nodded at the balding sheriff standing at the back of the wooden platform. He counted at least five rifles and more holstered revolvers than he'd seen on the entire trip. The deputies all looked uneasy but sharp-eyed, and he began to breathe easier.

Caroline's voice carried well. "It is not only voting rights that women are denied. Women cannot serve on juries. Or run for office. Or…"

Hawk hadn't known about all those things a woman couldn't do. All his life he'd been concerned only with what a woman *could* do— cook, keep house, bear children. And make a man happy.

He thought again about his mother. Had those things been enough for her, living as Luis Rivera's wife? Raising his son?

An ache lodged under his breastbone. What about Whitefern? Had his wife been unhappy living with him in town instead of with her tribe in Black Oak Canyon? She couldn't have voted anyway, being Cherokee. But what about all those other things?

His mind snapped back to Marguerite Rivera. His father had idolized his mother, but then why had she run away? Why? And Whitefern had gone with her. Why?

Questions from the crowd were starting. Hawk strained his ears to hear those voiced from the back of the gathering.

"Why would a happy married woman wanna vote, anyway? Ain't as if she's gonna care about who runs for sheriff, or even president."

Caroline fielded the queries with more polite good humor than he would have, given how simpleminded some of the comments were. After she had spoken for over an hour, she spied the pitcher of water left for her on the podium behind her. Still talking, she backed up toward it, then turned to reach for the glass.

The next thing Hawk knew she gave a cry and the pitcher crashed onto the floor. In an instant Hawk was beside her, his Winchester aimed into the crowd.

Unable to speak, she pointed under the water glass. Hawk caught her shoulder and pulled her hard against him, then glanced down at the podium.

A square of white paper lay where the pitcher had rested. Printed across it in black crayoned letters were five words: "YOU ARE GOING TO DIE."

"Sheriff Donovan," Hawk yelled.

"Yo," came a voice from under the trees.

"Search everyone. Look for a black crayon."

He turned Caroline's shuddering frame into his arms. "Easy. Take it easy. It's all right. Nobody's gonna get to you."

One of the deputies leaped onto the stage behind them and Hawk gradually moved Caroline toward him.

"She all right, Rivera?"

"So far. Escort us to the hotel, will you?"

"Sure thing." The wiry young man looped his free arm around Caroline's shoulders and together he and Hawk walked her across the square and up the seven whitewashed steps into the hotel.

"I—I'm all right," Caroline managed. She kept repeating the words until Hawk unlocked the door to their room, signaled dismissal to the deputy and moved her inside. The moment the door closed, she pressed her face into her hands and burst into tears.

"What the hell? Caroline? *Caroline?*"

He dropped the rifle onto Fernanda's bed and wrapped her in his arms, rocking her to and fro.

"Where is Fernanda?" she sobbed.

"With Sheriff Donovan. I asked him to look after her if anything happened."

"Hawk?"

"Yeah?" He could barely stand the anguish in her voice.

She sniffled. "Hawk, are you hungry?"

He jerked as if he'd been shot. *"What?"*

"I s-said, are you hungry? Hawk, I'm scared and tired and…hungry. I can do nothing about being scared or tired, but—"

Hawk stepped back and stared at her. "Yeah, I could eat something. Wait a minute."

He took his handkerchief out of his back pocket and mopped the tears off her cheeks. Then he turned her toward the door and stopped.

"You forgot your hat."

"No, I didn't," she said with a choked laugh. "I decided I don't like it anymore."

Well, hell. If she didn't want to be sassy, what *did* she want?

He was afraid to ask.

Chapter Thirteen

Caroline couldn't really eat much because she could not stop crying and kept laying down her fork to blow her sniffly nose. Apparently unbothered, Hawk managed to down half a roast chicken and three helpings of mashed potatoes swimming in gravy.

"I am such a coward," she said, twisting her handkerchief in her lap.

"Whoa." Hawk paused, a forkful of green beans on the way to his mouth.

"Well, I am," she pursued. "I am not the least bit brave. I don't know how Mama managed to keep going."

"Your momma wasn't being stalked. And since we're talking about bravery, let me tell you something I learned before I was out of short pants. Being brave doesn't mean you're not afraid. Being brave is when you're scared out of your skin but you move forward anyway."

Her eyes filled with tears. Aw, hell, he'd kill the bastard who left that message.

"Caroline, do you have any idea who might want to hurt you?"

She shook her head. "No one ever threatened Mama in this way. It started after she died and I was carrying on alone."

He gestured at her untouched plate. "Might as well finish your dinner. Then I've got another question for you."

"Ask me now. I hate suspense, Hawk."

"Get used to it," he said. "I'm not about to bring up this subject in public."

Her eyes widened into two huge purple-blue pools Hawk thought he might drown in if he wasn't careful. He dropped his gaze to his roast chicken and tore off a drumstick. Watching Caroline poke at her mashed potatoes wrung a chuckle from his too-dry throat.

Still, she determinedly shoveled in tiny bites until the mound on her plate had shrunk by half.

"Want some more tea?" He signaled the waitress hovering near the kitchen. When she drew near, she leaned over near his ear.

"Sheriff Donovan would like to speak with you, sir."

"Sure. Ask him to join us."

Caroline pushed her chair back. "I'll just leave you to—"

"Like hell." He didn't look up, just grasped her forearm. "Sit."

Sheriff Donovan slid his bulk onto an extra chair and hitched it up to the table with a tired sigh. "Afternoon, ma'am."

"Find anything?" Hawk asked.

"Nope. No crayons. No pencils. Not even any schoolkid's chalk."

Hawk nodded.

"Know what I think?" Donovan tipped his balding head toward Caroline. "I think that note got wrote out beforehand. Whoever done it waited until that pitcher of water got set in place and then that note got slipped underneath at the last minute."

Hawk nodded shortly. "Yeah."

The sheriff lowered his voice. "If I was you, Rivera, I'd take the lady and skedaddle."

"Yeah," Hawk said again. "Thanks."

The sheriff got to his feet. "Skedaddle," he repeated. He touched two fingers to his hat brim. "Ma'am."

Caroline clanked her teacup onto the china saucer. "I'm not going to ske—"

"Upstairs," Hawk interrupted.

They met Fernanda in the hallway outside the hotel room. "I go light more candles, *señor.*"

"Not yet," Hawk said. "I spied some cherry brandy behind the bar last night. Could you get it and bring it up to the room?" He slipped a bill into her hand. "Buy all the candles you want with the change."

He unlocked the door to their room. "Pack up your trunk," he ordered.

"What? But the train doesn't leave until—"

"Forget the train for now. I want you to sit

down and hear me out about something. Two somethings," he amended.

She perched on the edge of her bed. Hawk paced to the window and back until Fernanda returned with the brandy and three glasses; then she slipped out to visit the church again.

From the window he watched the Mexican woman cross the street. When her long black skirt disappeared into the wooden doorway, he uncorked the brandy and sloshed two hefty slugs into each tumbler.

Tentatively Caroline touched her tongue to the liquid. It stung like fire, but it tasted sweet and rich, like ripe cherries. Hawk tossed his back in a single gulp and poured another.

When she had downed about half her brandy he lifted the glass out of her hand, set it on the carpet beside the bed and hunkered down in front of her.

"Two things," he reminded. "First, about your speech-making."

She stiffened. "What is wrong with my speech-making?"

"Nothing's wrong with it. Hell, I'm halfway convinced by what you say myself."

She sent him a smile that made his joints melt. "Then what is it?"

Hawk exhaled on a sigh. "I think you're running on borrowed time. In fact, I think you're out of time. If someone can get close enough to you to slip a note under your water glass, sooner or later that someone is going to do more than connect."

"Connect?" Her voice sounded breathy. Maybe it was the brandy. Most likely it was gut-deep fear.

"Connect as in kill you."

She gave a little jump. "Oh." Once again those eyes of hers got so big he could swim around in them.

"So here's my first question. Can you be ready to leave tonight? There's a train going south at midnight."

"But I'm not going south, Hawk. I'm going west, to Washington Territory. To Huntington."

"I want you to go south. Back to Oakridge,

and then on to Gillette Springs. And then back to Smoke River."

"But why? I promised Mama... Hawk, I must continue."

"Well, Caroline, I'm asking you not to continue. I want to keep you safe, Caroline, but I can't do it with some kind of trap I can't even see closing in. In Smoke River, I..."

He took another swallow of brandy. "I can protect you in Smoke River. I know everybody in town, and I can get help from men I trust. I want to—God, this is hard to say. I want to set up a trap."

"Oh. I assume that is not so difficult. Why did you hesitate to tell me?"

"Because, Caroline, you're going to be the bait."

He snaked her glass up from the floor and pressed her fingers around it. "It's dangerous. But not as dangerous as riding blind in a territory I'm not familiar with, working with people I don't know."

She took a big gulp of the brandy. He could

tell when it went down because her eyes teared up.

"I would have to give up the speaking circuit Mama and I had planned."

"Yeah."

"The one I promised her I would complete after she died."

"Yeah."

She looked straight at him. "I won't do it."

"Caroline, look at it this way. Do you want to end up maybe changing a few minds, or even a lot of minds? Or do you want to end up dead?"

He thought she'd gone white before; now she looked like a damn ghost. He got to his feet and paced around the room while she just sat there on the bed, nursing her brandy.

"Well?" he said when he couldn't stand it any longer. He squatted on his heels before her.

"Yes," she murmured. "I want to live."

Thank you, Lord.

"Now," she said in an unnaturally calm tone, "what is your second 'something'?"

He held her gaze and prayed she wasn't

going to bolt. "I want you to tell me why you slapped me last night."

She tried to look away but he reached up and caught her chin, turning her face back toward him.

"I—I cannot."

"Yeah, you can."

"No."

"Try, dammit."

"I—it has nothing to do with you. I swear it."

"For that I'm damn grateful. But I still want to know—what *does* it have to do with?"

She tried to look everywhere but at him, but again, he didn't let her escape. His fingers kept gently returning her gaze to his; even when her eyes overflowed he made her look at him.

"It has to do with another man," she said finally.

"I figured something like that. Want to tell me about it?"

"No," she said quickly. Too quickly.

"Yes," he breathed. "Tell me what happened."

"He…he was bigger than I was. Stronger." She shook her head and shut her eyes tight. Hawk knew what was coming. His gut clenched, but he kept his hand against her chin and didn't move.

"This man, he…he forced me."

He didn't move, just waited. Her breathing grew more ragged, and then she was gulping back sobs.

"I was only t-twelve. He held me down and…and…"

He slid onto the bed beside her and wrapped both arms around her. Her brandy sloshed over onto his jeans but it didn't matter.

"And that's why you can't stand for a man to touch you. Kiss you."

She made an inarticulate sound against his shoulder.

"Who was it, Caroline?"

She shook her head violently and tried to break free. With one hand he pressed her head into his neck.

"Someone you knew?"

She gave a cry and wrenched away from him. Deliberately he brought her back within the circle of his arms.

"Someone you knew?" he repeated in a whisper.

Suddenly she tipped her head back and looked into his eyes. "It was my father."

Stunned, Hawk stared at her. "God damn him," he said, his voice quiet. "God damn him to hell."

She twisted away, but he held on. "Did your mother know?"

She shook her head, her mouth working.

"Does Fernanda?"

"No." Her voice was so faint he had to strain to hear.

"Only you know."

"And then what?" He was afraid to ask, but he knew he had to finish it.

"I shot him."

Chapter Fourteen

Hawk stared at her. "My God, you killed him?"

"I did, yes."

"I thought you'd never touched a gun before. You didn't even know how to cock my revolver, much less aim it."

"You are right… I did not. Papa always carried a pistol hidden under his vest. That night I— He came at me again. I screamed and he pulled out his little pistol, and when I grabbed for it…"

"It went off," Hawk supplied.

"The bullet hit his chest," she said, her voice almost inaudible. "And then he was dead. I never told a soul. I just left him there."

Hawk felt something rip inside his chest. God. He reached for her, but she flinched away.

"Mama never knew what he had done to me. Or what I had done. She took me away and I never told her."

He clenched his jaw so hard his teeth ached. And she couldn't escape her father because the law didn't allow her mother to have her. No wonder she was afraid to be touched. He wondered if she would ever forget.

As Hawk directed, Caroline began to lift her garments out of the wardrobe and pack them into the trunk. When Fernanda returned, he stepped out of the room on an errand of his own, and Caroline bolted the door from the inside.

When he reappeared he dangled a different room key in his hand. "Finish packing," he instructed. "But—" he tipped his head toward Caroline "—save your boy's disguise."

Fernanda snapped the trunk closed, and he dragged it out into the hallway. "Come on," he said, flashing the new key. "We're moving."

"But, *señor*, one new room, it is not enough?"

"Whoever is watching us knows we're in this room. If we move, he won't know where we are."

He manhandled the trunk to the far end of the hall and left it at the head of the stairs, then unlocked the door to a different room on the opposite side and ushered them inside.

"Fernanda, I want you to make one more visit to the church and talk to the padre."

"*Ay de mi*, the padre, he grows tired of me!"

Hawk drew the Mexican woman aside and spoke so quietly Caroline could not hear. Fernanda sent him a conspiratorial look and marched out the door; she returned a short time later with something bundled up under her black wool shawl.

"Now," Hawk said to Caroline, "I need you to put on those boy's duds you wore when we rode out of Smoke River."

Her eyebrows shot up. "May I ask why?"

"Nope. Don't ask—just get them on."

Three hours later, the two hotel porters found the trunk right where Rivera said it would be. They upended it, muscled it down the staircase and stowed it behind the registration desk. In the morning they would load it onto a cart, roll it to the train station, and heave it onto the Union Pacific bound west for Washington Territory.

A little before midnight, two priests in long black cassocks and a young boy in plaid shirt, jeans and leather boots slipped out the back door of the hotel and made their way to the train. The tall priest stepped into the station house, purchased three tickets and sent off a telegram.

When he emerged he studied the deserted passenger platform. Finally, with a nod of satisfaction, he ushered the other two travelers on board the southbound train, and the locomotive chuffed off down the track back to Oakridge.

Hawk settled into his seat and pulled the rifle from under his cassock. The other priest, short and pudgy in build, produced a large box lunch and a small flask of whiskey.

Fourteen hours later the southbound train

pulled into the station at Oakridge. Perched on the stagecoach waiting at the edge of the platform, Jingo Shanahan waved his battered hat at the three passengers who stepped down off the locomotive.

"Over here, Haw—uh, Father. Where's yer trunk?"

The tall priest laughed. "On its way to Washington. Good to see you, Jingo." He ushered his two companions into the waiting stagecoach, shut the passenger door, then climbed up next to the driver and laid his rifle over his knees.

"Kinda funny, seein' ya in them clothes," Jingo confided. "But yer deputy made it real clear what I's to do, so—" he spat tobacco juice off to the side "—here I am. Jes' gives me the jollies seein' you dressed up like a—"

"Just drive, Jingo."

The whip cracked and the stagecoach lurched forward. At Gillette Springs they stopped at the livery stable to pick up the horses Hawk had boarded. Then he folded up the black cassock and stashed it in his saddlebag, roped the mares behind his gelding and swung himself into the saddle.

By the time the stage, Hawk and the horses reached Smoke River some eight hours later, it was just before midnight and the main street was deserted. That was odd, Hawk thought. Unless his deputy had taken an added precaution and cleared out the downtown area. He didn't care what ruse Sandy had managed; he was just grateful no one would witness their arrival. Better yet, no one would know the whereabouts of Caroline MacFarlane until he was ready to spring his trap.

"Turn at the corner," he directed the stage driver.

At the door of his half sister's boarding-house, Hawk signaled a stop. Jingo pulled the team to a halt and waited until the large priest and the skinny kid inside climbed out and tip-toed up onto the wide front porch. At a signal from Hawk, he lifted the traces and the coach rolled away down the street and on out of town.

Hawk tapped on the dingy front door. "Ilsa?"

The door cracked open. "Hawk?"

"Yeah, it's me. Open up."

A tall, slim woman in a shabby night robe flung open the door and reached to hug him. "Oh, Hawk, I've been so worried! Sandy told me—"

He patted her shoulder. "Everything's under control, sis. Like I said, I've brought you two more boarders." He tipped his head toward Fernanda and Caroline, waiting on the steps behind him.

"A priest?" Ilsa's voice rose in surprise. "Hawk, Sandy didn't say anything about—"

Fernanda stepped forward. "You will forgive, *señora*? *Señor* Hawk does not tell everything."

The tall woman laughed. "I see my brother still hasn't changed. Even when he was a boy, he—"

Hawk cut her off. "Got anything to eat?"

"Of course. Come in. Eggs and bacon all right? And Elijah made ginger cookies this afternoon."

Hawk conducted Fernanda and Caroline

through the screen door Ilsa held open. He didn't introduce them.

The first thing the Mexican woman did was wriggle out of the priest's cassock. "I do not think the padre like being buried under all this black." She handed the fabric to Ilsa. "You can sew? Good for mourning dress."

Caroline had not spoken a single word since leaving the stagecoach. Now she was swaying on her feet. Hawk grasped her arm.

"You all right?" he said in a low tone.

She touched her temple. "Just a headache."

He walked her to an overstuffed chair. "Ilsa, you have anything for a headache?"

"Why, of course. You think I run a boarding-house unprepared for emergencies? Look in the cabinet next to the sink while I gather some eggs."

Caroline's head drooped. "I—I thank you for your kindness, Mrs....Rowell, is it?"

Ilsa propped work-worn hands on her hips. "As usual Hawk has forgotten to make introductions," she said with a fond smile. "I am Ilsa Rowell, Hawk's sister."

Hawk snorted. "I didn't forget, sis. Just figure sometimes it's best not to know."

"Nonsense," Ilsa retorted. "I'm waiting."

She had green eyes, like Hawk's, Caroline noted. But not as penetrating. And the woman's skin was three shades lighter than his.

Hawk swallowed. "Ilsa, this is Caroline…" He hesitated.

"Miss? Or Missus?" Ilsa asked, eyeing her boy's attire.

"M-miss."

"Hawk, get the girl some aspirin. And some coffee. It's on the stove."

"And her companion is Fernanda Sobrano. *Señora*, I think."

Fernanda's black eyes snapped. "Certainly it is *señora*. Except for you, *Señor* Hawk, men are worthless."

"Now wait a damn—"

"I am Fernanda Elena Maria Sobrano," the Mexican woman announced. "And, *por favor*, I also would be grateful for some café."

Ilsa pointed to the stove. "Brother, you are a fine sheriff, but as a host…"

"Please do not berate him, Mrs. Rowell," Caroline interrupted. "Hawk has saved my life on three occasions."

"As well he should," Ilsa said. She went on talking as she stalked out the back door, and her voice faded into the squawking of disturbed hens.

In her absence, Hawk shook some white tablets into his palm, poured coffee into a chipped mug from the sideboard and moved to Caroline, seated in the parlor. She clutched the aspirin and nodded her thanks.

Hawk returned to the kitchen and poured coffee for Fernanda, then lifted an iron frying pan from the hook behind the stove, poked up the fire and sliced a dozen slabs of bacon from the side hanging in the pantry.

Caroline opened her lids when the back door slammed. She watched Hawk expertly crack eggs from the wire basket Ilsa held out, then splash a bit of milk into the bowl with them. She blinked in surprise. Caroline couldn't scramble an egg if her life depended on it.

This man was such a puzzle, a combination of steel-spined sheriff and gentle brother. Hawk Rivera was different from any man she had ever known. However, she admitted, she had never before allowed a man within ten feet of her; Hawk was an exception.

Fernanda bustled about the small kitchen laying out plates and forks and frayed gingham napkins as if she'd lived here all her life.

Caroline downed the aspirin with a swallow of coffee and waited for the pain to recede, listening to the comforting sounds in the small kitchen, the sizzle of bacon, the low voices of Hawk and his sister talking about inconsequential things—her son's paper delivery job, the upcoming dance at Jensen's barn, and the sharpshooting contest Hawk's deputy, Sandy, had arranged next Saturday.

She opened her eyes when Hawk laid a plate of scrambled eggs and bacon in her lap and pressed a fork into her hand. "Didn't think you could make it to the table," he murmured.

"N-no, I—"

"Eat. Ilsa says your room's all ready and nobody's gonna disturb you until noon tomorrow. Oh, I almost forgot. Sis says she'll leave some clean duds outside your door. Unless you'd rather wear jeans and boots?" With a chuckle he tugged her plaid shirt collar.

Tired as she was, Caroline laughed. "It would be more sensible to maintain my disguise, but I have to admit that I feel less female in jeans than I ever have in my life. And my feet will never get used to wearing boots!"

Hawk opened his mouth to say something about her being "less female," then thought better of it. The less said about his feelings on that score the better. For him, there was not one thing about Caroline MacFarlane that would ever be "less female," no matter what she was wearing.

He rejoined Fernanda at the table, but as he shoveled in eggs and toast he kept one eye on Caroline. She was a misfit out here in the West. Must have been in Texas, too. She belonged in a city, in a fine house with servants and books and—well, everything a little town in Oregon didn't have.

Fernanda touched his wrist. "My lady, she is all right, *señor*?"

"Yeah, I think so. Tired. Got a headache. But she's not frightened anymore."

"She is never frightened until her *madre* die of the lung sickness. Then she hide it and do her…how you say?…her 'must do.'"

"Her duty," Hawk supplied. "She sure has one helluva work ethic."

"*Que?* What is 'ethic'?"

"Something that drives her. Compulsion, like. Something that makes her go on giving speeches when she's dead tired and scared to death."

"Ah. You think she will recover from this 'ethic'?"

Hawk thought about it. Probably not, since he now knew that part of what had been driving her was killing her father. He figured she had to keep moving to keep that memory from swamping her.

"*Señor*, look." Fernanda nodded toward the boyish figure slumped on Ilsa's best upholstered chair. Hawk pushed back from the table and stood up.

Ilsa glanced up from her coffee. "Put her in the blue bedroom, Hawk. I'll put Fernanda next to her."

"You are kind, *señora*," Fernanda said. "I will help in house."

Hawk lifted the still-full plate off Caroline's lap and set it on the floor beside the chair. Then he slid one hand under her knees, hoisted her into his arms and started for the stairs. The blue bedroom was at the far end of the hallway.

He walked as slowly as he could. She felt so good held against his chest he didn't want to let her go. At the last room he dipped to turn the brass knob and kneed the door open.

A blue print quilt covered the narrow bed under the window. Ilsa had sewed it by hand one square at a time when she'd first found herself a widow. He laid Caroline on top of it and folded the sides up around her. Then he slipped off her too-large boots. Tomorrow he'd check whether she had any blisters.

It was damn hard leaving her there, her head flopped over in sleep. Every bone in his body wanted to stretch out beside her, feel her warmth and the softness of her body against him. *Watch it, Rivera! You've been there before and it didn't end well.*

Gently he straightened her neck on the goose-feather pillow, then with a suppressed groan he stood up and tiptoed out the door.

Chapter Fifteen

∽∽∾∽∾∽

Caroline jerked awake to the sound of someone chopping wood outside. It took her a moment to remember where she was, in Hawk's widowed sister's boardinghouse. She wondered who was chopping wood and stretched to look out the window.

He faced away from her, his back tanned to the color of chestnuts, the muscles rippling under his skin with every blow of the ax. He was beautiful to watch, hefting the ax and bringing it down square onto a chunk of wood. At each blow, four equal pieces of oak fell away from the chopping block.

She owed him her life, she thought suddenly. A few nights ago he had kissed her, and she had paid him back by striking him. Even now her cheeks burned in shame at what she had done. She had explained about her father, about why she had panicked when he touched her, but she had seen the hurt and resignation in his eyes and it haunted her still.

The ringing of the ax stopped and he turned toward the house, then lifted his shirt off the fence. Scars shone white under the sprinkling of dark hair on his chest, and three odd parallel lines slashed across his midriff. Caroline pressed her lips together. This man had known violence.

He strode across the bare dirt yard toward the back porch, putting his arms into the sleeves of the blue cotton shirt. "Billy?" he yelled. "Come fill your ma's wood box."

Billy? Who was Billy?

A scrambling of feet outside her door had her pulse skittering. "Coming, Uncle Hawk."

What was the youngster doing outside her door? She fervently hoped Billy was under twelve years old. Then she realized she was stark naked under the bedsheet. The last thing she remembered was eating scrambled eggs in the parlor downstairs. Someone had carried her up to this room, but, oh, heavens! Had that someone also undressed her?

She crept out of bed, splashed cool water on her face from the pitcher on the bureau, then peeked into the armoire for her clothes. Empty. No shirt. No jeans. And, bless the Lord, no boots!

She opened the bedroom door to call Fernanda and found a neat pile of folded clean clothes on the floor. A threadbare petticoat, a faded yellow seersucker skirt and a simple white lawn shirtwaist with a high collar but no lace. Everything was slightly too large and the skirt and petticoat were so long they brushed the floor, but she was grateful nonetheless. The garments smelled good, like sunshine. But, she realized suddenly, there was no camisole. Not even any underdrawers!

And she had packed her shoes in the trunk that had gone on to Washington. Back to the hated boots.

She pulled them out from under the bed

and stuffed her bare feet into them. Her breath hissed in. More blisters. Quickly she pulled the hated things off and kicked them back under the bed. That left her feet bare. But the skirt was so long no one would ever see.

Downstairs Fernanda was humming as she moved about the kitchen rattling pans and rolling out piecrust. Hawk sat at the painted wood table peeling apples with his pocketknife.

"Coffee's on the stove," he announced without glancing up. "Wait an hour and you can have pie for breakfast."

"Pie!"

"Sure. You think all I do is keep law and order?" He grinned at her, his teeth white against his dark skin. She was quite sure she had never seen him grin at her like that before. She would have noticed.

Ilsa stepped in from the back porch, soapsuds clinging to her forearms. "I see you found the clothes I sent up with Billy. I'm sorry there were no clean undergarments."

Hawk's grin widened. "You mean she's not wearing—?"

Ilsa smacked his shoulder with the back of her hand and Fernanda's rolling pin halted. "My lady, she no wear corset since you dress her like boy."

"Oh?" Hawk's green eyes darkened.

Caroline drew herself up as straight as she could manage in her blistered bare feet. "Yes, thank you, I would like pie for breakfast, and no, I am not wearing any—" she swallowed, then lifted her chin "—underclothes. I will wash out my things when—"

"I tossed them into the washtub with mine," Ilsa interrupted.

Hawk rose suddenly and bolted for the back door. "Gonna need more wood."

Fernanda and Ilsa exploded into giggles.

"I will help with the washing," Caroline announced.

"No, *mi corazón*," Fernanda said. "You finish peel apples for pie."

So she peeled all the apples heaped in the huge crockery bowl, sliced them up and piled them into the bottom crust Fernanda laid in the pie tin. Little by little, listening to the crack of

Hawk's ax in the backyard, the chatter of birds in the walnut tree and Fernanda's humming, Caroline felt her taut nerves begin to relax. She was safe here, at least for a little while. At least until Hawk sprang his trap and she would be the bait.

Sweaty from another hour spent splitting firewood, Hawk stopped to survey the mounting tower of oak destined for Ilsa's wood box. He could hear his sister's breathy whistling coming from the back porch, and he rolled his eyes. He'd never been able to teach Ilsa to do a proper job of whistling through her teeth; his half sister was too much their mother's daughter, and her father, Momma's first husband, had died before Ilsa was two years old.

He strode onto the back porch and upended a bucket of rinse water over his head and chest. He chuckled at his sister's squawk. "Hey, sis, you wouldn't want me smelling like a logging camp come suppertime, would you? Besides, I have to go back over to the sheriff's office."

Every few hours something in Smoke River needed straightening out, a saloon card game gone sour, a lost schoolkid, even keeping order at the Ladies Temperance Union meeting, though how a bunch of teetotaler women could get so riled up was beyond him. His deputy would appear to have coped well enough, but he needed to check in now he was back.

The bucket of cold water washed off the sweat, but it didn't cool down his thoughts. So Caroline wasn't wearing any underclothes, huh? Hell's handbasket, that made him sweat all over again.

Chapter Sixteen

Supper was agony. Caroline had not realized how much she distrusted people, especially people sitting close together around a kitchen table. Especially males. The other member of Ilsa Rowell's boardinghouse had lived there for the past seven years, but he was still a man, and a stranger.

Elijah Holst was older, bearded, with snapping blue eyes and a paunchy waistline, but no matter how kindly he looked at her, or how gently he spoke, she felt herself pulling into her shell. Unable to think of a thing to say, she sat staring at her plate.

"Might not look like it," Elijah was saying to Fernanda, "but these here fingers are talented." He held out both wrinkled hands for her inspection.

"*Si*? What can your ten fingers do that mine cannot, *señor*?"

"Oho!" Elijah grinned at Billy, Ilsa's son, who sat next to Fernanda gobbling his supper. "Tell 'er, Billy. And don' leave nuthin' out."

Twelve-year-old Billy dumped more mashed potatoes onto his plate and passed the crockery bowl to Caroline. "Well, let's see, now. Old Elijah—"

"Hold up, son!" Elijah snapped. "Ain't 'old' a'tall." Billy dropped his head to hide a grin. "Yeah, well, *young* Elijah there sets type over at the Sentinel office. Printer's devil, Miss Jessamine calls him."

"Damn—Darn right," the old man exclaimed. "Faster 'n a greased pig with them type sticks."

"And he makes pretty good sugar cookies," Billy added.

Elijah stared at the boy. "'Pretty' good? You mean damn—uh, darn good, don'tcha? You sure gobble up enough of 'em."

Caroline watched the exchange and tried to talk herself into eating at least some of the food Ilsa had heaped onto her plate.

"Where is Uncle Hawk?" Billy asked suddenly. Caroline wondered the same thing. She'd hardly seen him since this morning. Was he avoiding her?

"Hawk is over at the sheriff's office," Ilsa said quietly. "He'll eat his supper later."

Elijah attacked another chicken drumstick. "Not hardly anythin' of interest happenin' for the newspaper to take note of. Da—Darn near fell asleep on my stool this afternoon. Miss Jessamine let me go home early."

Caroline caught Fernanda's eye and breathed a sigh of relief. No news meant no trouble. And no trouble meant no one was stalking her; no one here was intent on doing her harm. She wondered if she would ever be able to calm her jangled nerves, even in a household as orderly and peaceful as Ilsa's.

With half an ear she listened to "Pass the peas" and "More coffee?" and then Fernanda's humming while the Mexican woman scrubbed the plates and cups at the sink. The other ear she kept cocked for the hooves of fast-moving horses or gunshots or… She didn't know what, exactly, just something that would shatter the quiet on this balmy, peaceful summer evening.

She busied herself wiping the plates and stacking them in the sideboard while Billy and Elijah bent their heads together over a checkerboard.

Ilsa made a fresh pot of coffee, and when the dishes were done, Caroline carried a mug out onto the front porch. Fernanda stayed inside; Billy had promised to teach her how to play checkers.

She perched on the top porch step and wrapped the yellow seersucker skirt about her knees to hide her bare feet. Tomorrow she would have clean socks and she would try the boots on again. She knew her blisters would hurt, but she couldn't go barefoot every day.

The air was soft and flower scented, and the breeze through the walnut branches cooled off the heat of the day. It was quiet. Tranquil.

Then why, *why* did she feel so uneasy?

There could not be a house safer than the one where the sheriff lived. The town was pretty, the few streets were tree-lined, the buildings nicely kept and the flowers… She drew in a gulp of honeysuckle-scented air. Oh, she did love the flowers.

Mama always had flowers, roses and peonies and bright scarlet poppies in the fall. She wondered why Ilsa's backyard was so stark, just bare dirt, with the one walnut tree next to the unpainted fence. Maybe she could plant— but, no. She would not be here long enough to see them bloom. Lost in thought, she sipped her coffee until heavy boots came up the steps.

"Supper over?" Hawk asked. He settled himself beside her and used his thumb to shove back his wide-brimmed hat. She wished he hadn't; those green eyes of his bored into her and made her chest feel tight. She started to hitch over to make room but he snaked out a hand and caught her arm.

"Stay. I don't bite."

"Yes, I realize that, but—"

"But I do kiss," he murmured. She heard

gentle laughter in his voice. The memory of his mouth on hers still made her stomach flip-flop; under the lawn shirtwaist her heart began to thrum.

"Yes, you did miss supper," she said to change the subject. "But there might be some cold chicken left."

He shifted his gaze from her face and studied the lower porch step. "Yeah. Most often I do miss supper. Ilsa always saves something for me."

"She is a good cook," Caroline offered.

"Wasn't always," Hawk said. "Grew up spoiled. Couldn't even boil coffee."

"Well, she certainly can now." She gestured at the mug clutched between her hands.

"Yeah. I taught her."

"You? Not her mother?"

"Nope. Our momma had money. And servants, when sis was little."

"And you did not?"

"Sure as hell didn't. My father was Momma's second husband. He owned lots of acres, but it was a pretty hardscrabble ranch. By the time I came along, Ilsa was grown and gone and…" He stopped and stared off at the purpling hills in the distance. "She married too soon."

"What happened?"

"She was widowed pretty young. I didn't much like the guy she married, but I was too young to do anything about it. And then a horse rolled over on him. After the funeral, Ilsa came out to Smoke River to scratch out a life for her and Billy. It was tough going until she opened the boardinghouse. Still tough going."

"She works hard, I notice."

"You'll also notice she lives pretty close to the bone. Billy helps some. And I do."

"Is that why you came to Smoke River? To help your sister?"

"Partly. Town needed a sheriff. I needed to get out of Texas. And sis, well, she needed me. Boardinghouse doesn't bring in a lot."

"Fernanda and I should be paying her rent."

"You are. I'm paying it."

"But I can afford—"

He turned toward her. "You're gonna need your money, Caroline. Think a minute. You don't get paid for making your speeches, do you?"

"Well, no. I have never needed money. Mama had some. She even had enough to pay Fernanda. And when Mama died, I inherited it."

"You ever wonder how long that money's gonna last?"

She didn't answer. Instead she pulled her skirt tighter around her knees. Too late she saw her bare toes peeking out from under the yellow seersucker skirt. Before she could tuck them back under her skirt, Hawk saw them.

"Whoa. What happened to your shoes? Boots, I mean?"

"My shoes are in Washington, thanks to you. I packed them in the trunk the night we left. My boots are under the bed upstairs."

"Blisters, huh?" Hawk tried not to smile. Caroline's bare toes were arousing, but right now he didn't want to think about the effect they were having on him.

"Um…"

He bent forward and grabbed one of her ankles. "Let's see."

Billy rattled the screen door behind them. "Uncle Hawk? You hungry?"

"You bet I am."

Caroline tried to jerk her foot out of his grasp but his fingers closed around her ankle.

"Billy, bring me some of your ma's foot salve, will you?"

"Hawk," she murmured. "Put my foot down."

"Not hardly," he said softly. "Opportunities like this don't come along every day."

"You will scandalize the boy!"

"'Bout time, I'd say. Kids grow up fast out here in the West."

She stopped wriggling. "Is that what happened to you?" She made her voice as severe as she could manage. In the silence the screen door whapped open and Billy stepped through and slipped a tube of something into Hawk's free hand.

"I'm beatin' Elijah at checkers." He disappeared back into the house.

"Now," Hawk said, "come here."

"Hawk, no." She tried to yank her foot out of his grasp.

"Relax. I'm not going to kiss you, just smear some of this stuff on your blisters. Now hold still."

She gave a little squeak but stopped struggling. His hand pushed her petticoat up and her breath caught. "Oh!"

"Yeah, you've got some blisters." He uncapped the ointment, squeezed some onto his forefinger, and spread it over her heel. "Feel good?" Again, his voice held a smile.

She didn't seem to have enough air in her lungs to answer. The touch of his fingers on her skin was exquisite. Breath snatching.

He smoothed and caressed his hand over her skin and she bit her lip to keep from moaning aloud. Never had a man touched her like that. It was—it was—delicious. Unnerving. She never wanted him to stop.

"Sure got quiet all of a sudden," he said.

Caroline swallowed. "I am…thinking."

"Yeah? What about?" He released her foot and lifted the other one.

Oh, heavens, don't even ask! "N-nothing."

"You make a lousy liar, Caroline, you know that?"

"Yes. I mean no. I was thinking about your sister's backyard."

He nearly dropped her foot. "What?"

"Do you think she would let me plant some flowers back there?"

"Flowers, huh? You like flowers?" He traced his finger around and around her ankle.

"I do, yes. Roses, especially."

He wrapped her entire foot in his warm, strong hand, and she felt her cheeks heat. Her whole body was bursting into flame. All at once his motion stopped, but he did not release her.

"You feel like slapping me?"

"N-no."

"How come? I'm touching you."

"You are not frightening me."

"Yeah?" He captured her gaze and she found she could not look away.

"You care to tell me what I *am* doing to you?" he breathed.

"Hawk," she whispered, "this is scandalous."

His soft laugh surprised her. "You said that before. God, I thought maybe you didn't notice."

This time Caroline laughed. "Oh, I noticed all right. I am surprising myself."

"Good." He drew in a careful breath. "I'm afraid to ask whether you're wearing any underclothes."

"Hawk!" She smacked the hand cradling her foot. "How dare you ask me that?"

"Easy." He lifted her coffee mug out of her fingers, then grabbed her hand, folded it into a small fist and covered it with his own. "Been thinking about it all day."

She jerked and tried to stand up, but he wouldn't release her. She aimed her palm at his cheek, but he ducked.

With relief Hawk noted she was half sputtering and half laughing. He dropped her foot, grasped her elbows and pulled her up. "In what way are you surprising yourself?"

She smoothed down her skirt. "I have never... I have never wanted to be this close to a man."

Hawk held his breath for a good half minute. "And?"

"And," she said, her voice so soft he could scarcely hear it. "I—I find that I am liking it."

He felt like kissing her, but he didn't want to push his luck. He wanted to touch her all over, hold her, not like he'd done when she was scared or crying, but like a man does when he holds a woman in his arms. When he wants her.

His guts turned into cement. Oh, no. *No, by God.* He wasn't going to touch her. And he'd try like hell not to want her. One thing led to another, and before he knew it he'd be in love with her, and he knew he could never, never risk caring about a woman again. He had scars so deep inside from when Whitefern was killed he'd never even come close to probing anywhere near them.

"Uncle Hawk," Billy called from behind the

screen door, "Ma says come eat now or go hungry."

Caroline shoved him toward the boy. "Go. Fernanda made apple pie for dessert."

Apple pie? What the hell did that have to do with temptation?

Maybe everything. It was all craving, right? It was all about hunger. And, oh, boy, right about now he had more than a man-sized load of that.

Just what he was going to do about it was a question he couldn't begin to answer.

Chapter Seventeen

~~~~~~~~

"You goin' to the big competition today?"
Across the breakfast table, Elijah's blue eyes
rested on Caroline with a question.

"Well, I—"

"Sure she is," Billy said, his mouth full of
oatmeal. "Uncle Hawk's gonna beat ever'body."

"Beat them, how?"

Elijah snorted. "He's gonna outshoot all
those fancy-ass ranch hands that thinks it's
a big deal to plug a rattlesnake at ten paces."

She cringed inside. "You mean it's a contest
of firearms?"

"You don't much like guns 'n' shootin', do
ya, missy?"

Like it! She hated even the thought of firing a gun. What if Elijah knew she had shot and killed her own father? What if Ilsa knew?

She wondered if Ilsa could fire a gun. Her pistol rested in the bottom bureau drawer upstairs, wrapped up in her jeans, and she knew Fernanda always carried hers in the pocket of her voluminous black skirt.

At the moment the two women were out in the backyard, hanging men's denims and shirts on the clothesline. "No, Eli, I think I will not attend the competition."

"C'mon, Miss Caroline," Billy begged. "I bet Hawk'd want someone else rooting for him besides me and Eli."

She wanted to watch him, it was true. She wondered if he was truly as good a shot as Billy seemed to think.

A shiver crawled up her spine. When Hawk sprang the trap he'd talked about, could he really keep her from getting killed?

"Where will this contest be held?"

"Out in back of the jail," Eli supplied. "In a big empty field. Lotsa room for spectators. I kin walk ya on over there after breakfast."

Half an hour later, Caroline and the old man set off down the street. Despite two pairs of clean socks and Hawk's application of salve the night before, she winced at every step. Boots, she decided, were most definitely not for ladies.

Billy danced ahead along the board sidewalk, but she was grateful for Elijah's halting gait. "Rheumatiz," he confessed. "Slows me down."

She didn't mind in the least. It gave her a chance to study the downtown area in more detail than she'd been able to on her first visit, when she had spoken to the townspeople about women's suffrage and Hawk had thrown his body over hers when someone shot at her.

Now she noticed the businesses along the main street, Ness's Mercantile with bushel baskets of peaches displayed in front, Poletti's Barbershop, Uncle Charlie's Bakery. Even a dressmaker. Self-consciously she looked down at the worn seersucker skirt Ilsa had lent her. Soon she would need her own clothes.

Eli steered her through a narrow alley between the jail and a livery supply shop and they emerged at the edge of a huge sunbaked field of tall grass, already thronged with people. Caroline hesitated. What if someone...?

As if he could read her mind, Eli patted her arm. "Now don't you worry none, missy. Hawk's got his deputy and the Federal marshal, Matt Johnson, watchin' over ya."

She recognized the lanky blond deputy, Sandy, who had walked over from the jail after breakfast just that morning for a cup of Ilsa's coffee. Eli pointed out the tall marshal standing off to one side of the field. Sunlight glinted off his leaf-shaped badge but his hat rode so low his face was obscured. She hoped his eyes were sharp.

"An' that's not all," Eli continued, guiding her to a shady spot under a spreading maple tree. "Yonder's Rooney Cloudman, an' standin' next to him is Colonel Wash Halliday, the feller he used to track for in the army."

Caroline studied both men. They carried rifles, as did all the contestants, but she noted that Rooney, an older man in a weather-worn

Stetson, kept his index finger curled around the trigger of his weapon. Colonel Halliday, tall and rangy with a touch of gray in his mustache, held his rifle loosely at his side, the barrel pointing toward the dry grass. The colonel was bareheaded, she noted. In fact he was the only man in the entire crowd without the wide-brimmed hat men out here in the West seemed to favor.

She searched for Hawk and found him near the marked-off firing line, deep in conversation with a whip-thin, dark-skinned man with eyes that missed nothing.

"That's Jericho Silver," Eli said. "Useta be the sheriff afore Hawk came. Now he's the district judge. Man's a fine shot. Jericho's gonna make it tough for Hawk to win. When Jericho's not competing," Elijah added, "he'll be guarding."

"Guarding? You mean me?"

Eli snorted. "Hell's tail feathers, girl, you think Hawk's gonna let you wander around town without someone watchin' out for ya?"

Caroline said nothing, but a warm feeling of being protected flowed over her. *Hawk was watching out for her.* And he had friends who were doing the same. *I know everybody in town, and I can get help from men I trust.*

"Eli, if I wanted to visit the dressmaker tomorrow, would one of Hawk's friends mind accompanying me?"

"Count on it. Hawk ain't lettin' ya out of his sight, one way or t'other."

The warmth in her chest blossomed. *I owe you my life, Hawk Rivera. Thank you from the bottom of my heart.*

The first competitors arranged themselves in a ragged line halfway across the stubbly field, about fifty yards from the target, which was a playing card nailed to a tree stump. A queen of hearts, Caroline noted. When Hawk or the marshal or Colonel Halliday stepped up to the firing line, she noted that the other four men either kept their gazes riveted on her or continuously scanned the swelling crowd. Still, she felt vaguely uneasy.

"Eli, do you know everyone in town?"

"Sure do. Why?"

"Do you see anyone here you don't recognize? A stranger?"

His sharp blue eyes studied the onlookers gathered under the maple tree and in the open field beyond where the target was set up. "Nope. All Smoke River gents. An' ladies," he added. "That there's Maddie Silver, the one with two babes in that push-cart thingamabob with wheels. Colonel Halliday's wife, Jeanne, she's standin' next to Maddie. Billy's half-sweet on her daughter, Manette."

"I am not!" Billy grumbled from behind them. "Teddy MacAllister is sweet on her. She's stuck up, always talkin' French. He can have her for all I care."

Eli surreptitiously bumped Caroline's arm. "What'd I tell ya?" he murmured. "Sweet as molasses candy."

Caroline studied the girl in the crisp white pinafore. Had she ever been that young? Had anyone ever been sweet on her?

Instantly a crushing blackness descended. *Papa.* Papa had ruined her, had driven away her innocence, her belief in everything that mattered. Her father had destroyed something inside her just as surely as she had killed him that awful night back in Boston. She shuddered and shut her eyes tight.

"What's the matter, girl?" Eli intoned. "You see somethin'?"

"N-no. Just a—a bad memory." The instant the words left her lips she went cold all over. Except for Hawk, she had never told anyone about her father. Somehow even thinking about what had happened made it real all over again.

Oh, God, she would never be normal. A man, even one as strong and understanding as Hawk Rivera, would never be able to get close to her. She would always, always react with an instinctive need to fight him off.

"Watch now, missy," Eli urged. "They're startin' the competition."

Part of her couldn't watch. She hated the sound of gunfire. Hated the knowledge of what a bullet could do. But another part of her couldn't keep her eyes off Hawk as he strode forward to the chalk line in the dirt. He thumbed back his gray hat, raised the rifle and held it steady for so long she found herself holding her breath.

Fire it. Just pull the trigger and get it over with.

Unconsciously she felt for the pistol she'd stuffed into her skirt pocket before leaving the house. Hawk had made her promise to carry it with her wherever she went, even out to the backyard to hang up wet laundry.

She noticed a gangly girl about twelve, dressed in an ill-fitting gingham dress, circling behind the crowd and devouring Hawk with avid eyes. "That's Noralee Ness, the mercantile owner's girl," Eli volunteered. "Sets type for the *Lake County Lark*. She's got it kinda bad for Hawk, I guess. Makes big mooney eyes ever' time he walks past."

"Isn't she a little young?"

"Ain't no right age to fall in love, missy. Hawk'll tell ya that."

"Oh?"

Elijah clammed up.

Intrigued, Caroline turned to him. "What is the right age, Elijah?"

"Ain't my place to speak of it," he muttered. "He'll tell ya hisself when he's ready. Or…"

"Or?" she prompted.

"Or he won't."

What was "it"? she wondered. She watched the girl, Noralee, press her back against the tree they were all standing under, her adoring gaze on Hawk's tall form at the firing line. She felt halfway sorry for her, wearing her heart so blatantly on her sleeve.

Hawk put a bullet a scant inch from the heart in the center of the card, wiped the sweat out of his eyes with his shirtsleeve, reloaded and sent a second shot smack through the first hole.

"Off your game a bit, Hawk?" Jericho Silver said with a laugh. "Audience never bothered you before."

"Doesn't now," Hawk said.

"No? Then how come you keep looking over at that tree behind us? Someone you tryin' to impress?"

"Shut up, Jericho."

Jericho chuckled. "Thought so. Gal in the yellow skirt, right? Real pretty."

"Never gave her a second thought," Hawk lied.

"Thought that once about Maddie, too. Damn dumb thing for a man to do." Jericho stepped up to the firing line, shouldered his rifle and put another hole squarely through Hawk's.

"She the one you're protecting, right?" Jericho said as he reloaded. He shot again, this time drilling a mark an inch the other side of the bull's eye.

Hawk didn't answer. Jericho Silver knew everything that went on in Smoke River, which farmer was quarreling with what rancher, who was stealing someone else's woman, who was watching who's back. He knew Jericho was watching his, same as he watched Jericho's when the need arose. The man wasn't the Smoke River sheriff any longer, but he was a damned reliable friend, even if he was the town judge.

"How long is she going to be in town?" Jericho stepped aside to let Wash Halliday take his position.

"Long enough to catch the bastard who's trying to kill her," Hawk growled.

"Got any leads?"

"Not a damn one. I told you, it's someone who hates the idea of women getting the vote."

"I felt that way once," Jericho said in a conversational tone.

"Yeah? What changed your mind?"

"Maddie. And that set of law books she gave me for a wedding present. What about at night?" Jericho went on with no change in inflection.

Hawk jerked. "What about *what* at night?"

Hell. All kinds of things went on at night when it came to Caroline. His thoughts circled and backtracked, remembering the scent of her hair; the softness of her skin; her trim, tiny little ankles; and the way her eyes went wide when she was thinking. Or *said* she was thinking.

Jericho clapped him on the shoulder. "I mean who's guarding her at night while you're sleeping?"

"Sandy. And Rooney Cloudman. She's watched twenty-four hours a day."

And night. Goddamn, in the evening he couldn't stop looking at her across the supper table and he couldn't stop thinking about her at night from the time he crawled into his bed at the opposite end of the hall until the rooster crowed and he went over to the jail to relieve his deputy.

"Does she know?" Jericho asked quietly.

"Know what? That she's under surveillance?"

"No, you damn fool. That you're in love with her."

Hawk whirled on the man. "Jericho, I've never slugged a judge before, but so help me—"

"Watch it, Hawk. Here she comes." With a laugh Jericho sauntered off toward his wife and their twin boys.

Caroline was smiling. Lordy, he wished she'd stop. Her lips looked like ripe raspberries and he couldn't take his eyes off them.

"Is it over? Did you win?"

"No and no. That's only the first round. Didn't you see?"

"Well, some. I found it difficult. The noise of the guns, I mean."

Hawk stared at her. "But you came to watch m—" He caught himself. "The competition. Did you think it wouldn't bother you?"

Caroline looked away. "I came to watch you, Hawk. I forgot there would be so much gunfire." Her voice had a little tremor in it. How she wished she could hide it. She didn't *want* to be frightened around him.

But she was.

He grasped her arm and walked her over to where the slim, dark-skinned man and his wife stood. "Maddie, have you got any cotton?"

The attractive young mother looked up. "Cotton? You mean like a cotton ball? I will look in my bag. But first, introduce me to your companion. My goodness, for a sheriff, you have the worst manners!"

Hawk gestured awkwardly from Caroline to the young woman. "Caroline, meet Maddie Silver. Yeah, I need a cotton ball."

Maddie sent Caroline an amused look and rummaged in the large mesh bag she was carrying. "Don't tell Jericho," she whispered as she pressed a wad of cotton into her hand, "but I use a bit of this in my own ears at night when the twins…" She sent Caroline a wide smile.

"Come visit me, why don't you?" Maddie glanced at Hawk. "It's perfectly safe. I am a Pinkerton agent."

Caroline gaped at her until Hawk drew her off behind the thick tree trunk. "Stuff your ears full of this, Caroline. Just don't tell Eli you can't hear what he's rambling on about."

He laid his hand on her shoulder and squeezed gently. "But be sure and take it out when I get home for supper tonight. I've got something on my mind."

Chapter Eighteen

The competition continued until there were only two contestants left, Hawk and Jericho Silver, and the target was moved back another fifty yards. Hawk and Jericho each fired two rounds, and it seemed to her just one hole showed on the queen of hearts. "Whooee," Eli crowed. "That's mighty fine shootin', a rifle at one hundred yards."

Then they moved the target back another fifty yards, and each competitor shot only once; the first one who missed was judged the loser. Caroline could scarcely bear to watch.

Hawk lost. Jericho clapped him on the back and offered to buy him a beer, but Hawk shook his head, then looked for Caroline.

At supper that night Caroline couldn't sit still. *What* was it Hawk had on his mind? She fidgeted, knocked her knife onto the kitchen floor not once but twice and finally laced her fingers together in her lap to stop their fluttering.

Hawk didn't appear until halfway through the baked beans and corn bread, and then it got worse. When he strode in, his hair still wet from washing up at the pump out back, Caroline reached for a glass of water and knocked it over.

Fernanda sent her a questioning look. "*Hija*, you have an itch?" The Mexican woman's sly smile indicated she knew all about the nerves dancing up and down Caroline's spine.

"How come you didn't win today, Uncle Hawk?" Billy piped.

"Can't win all the time, Billy. You know that."

"*You* can," the boy insisted.

"Guess I was distracted." Hawk reached for the platter of corn bread and Billy shoved the butter dish across the table toward him.

"What distracted you, Uncle Hawk?"

"Billy," Ilsa admonished. "Let your uncle eat his supper."

Eli's blue eyes twinkled. "Mighta been the crowd, huh, Hawk?"

"Eli," Ilsa said in the same tone she used to caution her son. "Enough."

Across the table, Fernanda and Ilsa exchanged glances, and all at once Caroline wanted to scream. *What was going on that she didn't know about?*

She bolted for the kitchen, sank her plate and fork into the bucket of dishwater heating on the stove and fled to the backyard. The washing she had hung on the clothesline earlier that afternoon was now dry and flapping in the breeze.

Caroline grabbed the wicker laundry basket and began unpinning the garments and folding them up. She hadn't reached the second row of sheets before the screen door banged open and someone lifted the clothespin bag out of her hand.

"Bedclothes, huh?" He unpinned a pillowcase and dropped it into the basket.

"You should fold it up," she said. "Ilsa says it smooths out the wrinkles and saves ironing."

He unpinned another sheet. "I don't mind wrinkles."

"Well, you should. You'll sleep better on smooth—"

"Nothing's gonna help me sleep," he said mildly. "These yours?" He flicked his forefinger against the remaining sheet and a matching embroidered pillowcase as he unpinned them.

"Well, yes."

"Okay, let's fold this one up." He shook out the square of muslin and offered her two corners, then moved toward her and mated his corners to hers.

The intent look in his eyes made her belly flip-flop. "I can manage from here on."

He paid no attention, just smoothed the crease in the once-folded sheet and again offered her the corners. This time when they brought them together he captured both her hands.

"I need to talk to you."

"I need to fold up the laundry."

He barked a laugh. "Don't want to talk, huh?"

"It isn't that so much as…well, yes, it is that. I am just beginning to feel safe here at your sister's, and now I have a feeling you're going to spoil it."

She bent to retrieve the wadded-up sheet he'd tossed into the basket, but he jerked it out of her hand. "Dammit, why don't you listen first and then decide?"

She snatched the sheet back. "Because I don't want things to change. I'm just now starting to sleep at night without dreaming, and—"

"Caroline, you've got your head in the sand. If you think this problem is gonna go away, you'd better take another look at how close you came to not getting to Smoke River in one piece."

She was silent for so long Hawk wondered if she'd heard him. *Of course she heard you, you idiot. You're yelling at her!*

She stuffed the crumpled sheet back into the basket and spun away toward the back porch. But she didn't stomp through the screen door.

Instead, she settled on the wooden porch step and wrapped her skirt around her legs. It was the same yellow skirt Ilsa had loaned her three days ago; a splotch of applesauce had dried near the hem.

"Sooner or later you're gonna have to wash that skirt," he remarked.

"I can't. I have only jeans and one shirt to wear. I must visit the dressmaker."

He laughed softly, then settled on the step below her. "What about your underclothes?"

"What about them?" she snapped. Her cheeks got real pink. Damn pretty color.

"Just wondering."

"Wondering what?"

"Whether you're wearing any."

"Of course I am! Ladies should always wear undergarments."

"Not always," he said quietly.

Caroline had had enough of conversations that made her skin go hot and her stomach fill with grasshoppers. She tried to stand up, but he caught her hand and yanked her down.

"I want you to listen to me." His voice had

turned so hard it sent a shiver up the back of her neck. Hawk Rivera must be formidable as a lawman. Few would withstand an order given in that tone.

"All right, I am listening."

He picked up her hand, the same one he'd pulled her down with. "Did I hurt you?"

"It doesn't matter."

"Hell if it doesn't. I've never abused a prisoner in my care yet."

"A prisoner? *A prisoner?* I am most certainly not your prisoner!"

"Damn right," he replied. "But you're under my protection. It's the same thing."

"Is this what you wanted to talk about?" She made her voice as severe as she could manage, but the truth was that a conversation conducted while folding up laundry was so ludicrous it almost made her laugh. Mama would have found it hilarious. That is, if it were not so serious. Hawk was right. The situation as it was could not continue.

She noticed he was staring off toward the golden hills in the distance.

"Okay," he began. "Here's how I see it. You're hell-bent on traveling around making speeches. You ever think about stopping?"

"You mean give up working to get the vote for women? No, I could not give it up, Hawk. It is important."

"It would get you out of the line of fire."

"But this is my life's work! I can't just walk away because the path is rough."

"I was afraid you'd say that. Your path is more than 'rough,' Caroline. Your path is suicidal."

"But it will not be when you catch that man who—"

"What if I can't?" He scuffed his boot heel back and forth across the wooden step. "After the competition today I talked to the marshal, Matt Johnson. He made me see things a lot clearer. I've got five men guarding you, including me. That works only if you're here in Smoke River, but I don't think you want that, do you?"

"What about your stakeout plan? The one you talked about back in Boise?"

"It's too dangerous. Matt saw that right off."

"Could we try your plan anyway? I cannot live my life like this, compromising what I have set out to do and looking over my shoulder every time I make a speech."

Again he picked up her hand. "To be honest, Caroline, I'm afraid to try my plan. Any plan."

She stared at him. "Hawk, I would judge you as a man who fears very little."

"Maybe. But I'm sure as hell afraid of this. I'm afraid to put you at risk."

"Then it seems we are at an impasse."

Hawk groaned, then brought her hand to his lips. "Risk I can live with. Danger I can live with. But an impasse? Not hardly."

He twisted to wrap his fingers about the back of her neck and drew her face down to his. "Don't scream. I'm going to kiss you."

He levered his body up beside her and reached sideways to take her face between his two hands.

"Wait," she breathed.

"No."

"Hawk—"

He captured her words under his mouth, moved slowly, carefully over her lips until he felt her tremble and he broke away to gulp air. "Hell, Caroline."

"What is it?"

He blew out a heavy breath. "Just hell." He kissed her again, hoping to God she wasn't frightened, that she was liking it. Him. Her mouth was like hot silk, and he drank deep while his heart turned a slow cartwheel and floated up into his throat. *God help him.*

He lifted his head and looked into her eyes, now deep blue and shiny. Caroline brought her hand up to touch her trembling lips, then noticed that her fingers were trembling as well and buried them in the folds of her skirt.

"I—" she began again, working to keep her voice steady. "I would like…"

Hawk held his breath.

"I—I would like to visit the dressmaker tomorrow afternoon. Would you go with me?"

"What? That's all you can say?" Incredulous, he stared at her. "I kiss you until I'm burning up inside and all you want to talk about is the dressmaker?"

"Well, will you?" He thought he saw a fleeting smile cross her lips, but maybe it was just his imagination. Maybe everything was his imagination, her lips accepting his kiss, her fluttery breathing, the glow in her eyes.

"Hell, no, I won't."

Her eyes went wide. "Why not?"

"I don't think I can stand watching you get fitted for a dress or a skirt or whatever it is you need."

She laughed. "But Hawk. I'll just be getting measured. I won't be taking off my—"

He jolted to his feet, yanked all the rest of the washing off the clothesline and used the wicker basket to hide his body's unmistakable evidence of how damn much he wanted her.

Chapter Nineteen

⁓⁓⁓

The dressmaker, Verena Forester, was in her midforties, Caroline judged, with gray-streaked blonde hair and a sour expression. The woman was looking at her as if she had strawberries growing out of her ears.

"What kinda skirt, may I ask?"

"Something plain. A simple bombazine in a dark color, perhaps."

"Four gore or six?"

Caroline had to smile at the mystified expression on Hawk's face. He stopped pacing back and forth in front of the display window and planted himself at her side. "Gore?" he whispered.

"Gores refer to the fullness," she murmured.

"Make it with pockets," he ordered the dressmaker.

Verena blinked. "What on earth? Sheriff Rivera, do you always stick your nose into your..." she eyed Caroline, clearly suspicious of her supposed relationship to Hawk "...your *niece's* fashion choices?"

It was clear the dressmaker knew Caroline was not really his niece. "Yep," came Hawk's instant reply. "Carrie's got no sense of propriety, never has had. I'm here to keep her looking decent."

Verena's lorgnette fell to her almost-flat bosom and Caroline gasped. "Hush up!" she hissed.

"I won't have any bombazine until fall," Verena said smoothly. "But I do have a nice dark green poplin. Or perhaps royal blue?"

Undaunted, Hawk pressed on. "Pockets, like I said. Big ones."

"Just what," Verena said icily, "do you intend to put in them, miss?"

"A pist—"

"Pie tin," Hawk interjected. "Make them

big enough to hold a pie tin. And—" he drew Caroline over to a display of bright colored prints "—not dark green. Make it in—" he ran his forefinger over the cloth "—this one."

He pointed to a gaily flowered red-and-yellow calico, a color so bright Caroline would never consider wearing it.

Verena nodded her approval and lifted the bolt onto the counter. "For the dance on Saturday night, is that right?"

"What dance?" Caroline ventured.

"Why, the Jensen's barn dance," the dressmaker explained. "They hold one every summer."

Caroline noted the wistful look in the dressmaker's hazel eyes. She also noted that her cheeks turned rosy whenever Hawk looked at her. Heavens! Were half the females in Smoke River hankering after the sheriff?

"And make up another skirt in the dark blue, would you?" Caroline asked. "Also with pockets. Large ones."

The dressmaker smiled. "Need any petticoats? Or shirtwaists?"

"Oh, no. I don't, thank you."

"Yes." Hawk contradicted. "And add some lace here and there. Ilsa's clothes never have any lace."

Caroline gaped at him. "Ilsa probably cannot afford lace," she murmured. "And I don't want to dress like a peacock while under her roof."

Verena fingered another bolt of fabric. "How about this forest green muslin, made with flounces?" She whipped out a tape measure and measured Caroline's waist while Hawk watched avidly. She fervently wished he would spy some miscreant outside the window and leave her in peace. But she pivoted and lifted her arms on Verena's command while the sheriff's eyes darkened into emerald pools and his mouth pressed into a line.

Abruptly he stepped between the dressmaker and herself and drew her off behind a display of hats. "What about undergarments?" he intoned.

She gave a little squeak and Hawk grinned. "How dare you presume—" she whispered.

"Come off it, Caroline. Ilsa's two sizes bigger than you around the waist. Her bloomers are probably falling off your hips right this minute."

Hawk knew he shouldn't have said that, but it was worth it to watch Caroline's eyes grow larger and more purple-blue and her mouth drop open into a little pink O. Before she could explode, he walked her back to the counter and plunked down two bills.

"My, uh, niece and I don't see eye to eye on a lot of things," he said blandly. "So throw in a couple of petticoats and…whatever understuff she needs."

Verena was all smiles. "Your *niece*, Sheriff Rivera, is a very fortunate young lady."

Caroline shot him a look that could curl tree bark and marched out the door. Hawk peeled off another bill and tossed it on the counter. Verena looked from the money to Hawk and back to the money.

"When—?"

"By Saturday morning," he supplied. "Dance

is Saturday night." He caught up to Caroline before she reached the bakery next door.

"You are a very generous 'uncle,' Hawk. But really, I—"

"You don't like being taken care of, do you?"

"I don't like being bossed around."

"Better get used to it. Remember, *niece* Caroline, for all intents and purposes, you are my prisoner."

Caroline had never been to a country barn dance before. It was as unlike the Sunday afternoons at Miss Handley's Dancing Academy as Shasta daisies were from cheese. The music was deafening. Two guitars, a banjo, a skittery-sounding violin, and the oddest-looking bass fiddle she'd ever seen, part washtub and part broom handle. The stomping of cowboy boots on the plank floor raised enough dust to make old ladies along the sidelines sneeze into their lace-trimmed handkerchiefs.

Hawk leaned in close. "Nothing like Boston, huh?"

She shook her head. "It is most definitely not like Boston." She felt awkward and as out of place as a petunia in a cabbage patch. Everyone seemed to know everyone else. Her new flowered calico skirt was sinfully swirly, the most brightly colored garment she had ever owned. But she didn't want to stand out. She wanted to hide in the shadows. She almost wished for her familiar too-big boots instead of the proper black leather lace-ups she'd purchased at the mercantile.

"What's wrong?" Hawk whispered. "You look white as skimmed milk."

"I feel conspicuous."

He chuckled. "You are conspicuous. You're the prettiest woman here." His gesture took in the spacious wood barn and the crowd of people milling about.

Dumbstruck, Caroline stared up at him.

"It's true," he said. "I'm afraid to dance with you because sure as chickens lay eggs, the minute I take you out on the floor some local cowboy's gonna cut in."

She caught her breath. "Oh. Don't let them, Hawk. Please."

"You think I'm crazy? I wouldn't let another man get within fifteen feet of you. So, you'd better dance with me, Caroline. I figure it's the only way I'm going to get my arms around you for more than ten seconds."

He grabbed her hand and pulled her onto the floor, and the next thing she knew he was holding her close and moving to the thumping of the bass fiddle. Her heart began to hammer.

"Sorry if my holster is bumping against you," he said after a moment. "These days I wear it everywhere."

"I cannot feel it."

"Well, then, guess I'd better hold you a little closer," he said with a laugh. "You carrying your pistol?"

She nodded.

He tightened his arm across her back. "You sure? I can't feel it."

That made her laugh, half in outrage and half in amusement. Good heavens, underneath this tough, unflappable lawman exterior, Hawk Rivera was just a man like any other.

No, not like any other. Her breath stopped. Hawk was different, so different she had let him kiss her, not once but twice, and now she was letting him hold her close in his arms, feeling his breath stir her hair.

Expertly he fended off the men who wanted to cut in, keeping her back to them and swinging her away just as male after male sidled forward, arm raised to tap Hawk on the shoulder.

A glow of warmth spread through her chest. Hawk was protecting her from all of them.

She began to relax her stiff spine. He must have felt it because he pulled her even closer, so close that her nose brushed his muslin-clad shoulder. He smelled of wood smoke and something spicy and male that made her stomach feel funny.

She wasn't used to being held like this, face-to-face. It made her jittery. Apprehensive. It reminded her of…

She willed her mind to move elsewhere, to the chatter of people around them, the vio-

lin music that grew wilder and more uninhib-
ited than any violin sounds she'd ever heard.
She studied the children on the sidelines, and
the women, some young and smooth-skinned,
rocking babes against their breasts, and some
older with graying hair pulled into buns and
steel-rimmed spectacles, fanning themselves
with folded paper fans.

Hawk stopped angling her away from the
hopeful men at the edge of the dance floor,
and she prayed they had all given up.

He had also stopped talking. Instead he just
held her and let his body do the talking. His
hand at her back was warm and insistent, pulling her into his chest until her breasts touched
his shirt and the nipples tingled.

She realized she had never danced with a
grown man before. The gangly boys at the
dancing academy had never held her like this;
they scarcely knew how to move their huge,
clumsy feet. But she liked dancing with Hawk,
and that surprised her. She liked hearing his
breath pull in and out and grow ragged when

she looked up at him, liked feeling his heart thump under his blue shirt.

After an hour they stopped at the refreshment table, cobbled together out of two sawhorses and three two-by-twelve boards. Hawk ordered lemonade for her and beer for himself, and in his typical fashion he ignored making introductions. Maybe he didn't want her name too well-known around town. Or maybe Ilsa was right; Hawk had very rough manners.

She found she didn't care. Maddie Silver smiled at her from across the room, as did Jeanne Halliday, the mother of little Manette, the girl Billy insisted he was *not* sweet on. Eli was busy partnering Ilsa and then young Noralee Ness and then a beaming Fernanda, who danced with real verve.

It was unexpectedly pleasant being here, she decided, sipping her lemonade. But she knew it would all change when she spoke her piece to the townspeople and Hawk got ready to spring his trap. He'd told her he knew deep down it was the only way to catch her assailant.

Then people would begin to take sides and arguments would start, questions would erupt from hostile listeners. And all those men who now wanted to cut in on Hawk on the dance floor would yell insults at her and harangue against their wives or girlfriends for even listening to her.

But she had to do it. Someone, a lot of someones, must carry the message to everyone who lived in this great and good country so that they could all be truly free and equal. But the next time she gave a speech she would, as Hawk warned, be once again in the line of fire.

She downed two more cups of lemonade and tried to calm her nerves. Eventually Hawk guided her over to Marshal Johnson and his very pregnant wife, Ellie, and went in search of Jericho Silver. The instant he disappeared, Caroline noted that the marshal stepped away from his wife and stood apart, scanning the throng of dancers and onlookers, his hand resting casually on his holstered revolver.

Maddie Silver smiled and patted the bench beside her.

"Someone is always watching over you, Caroline. You need not worry when you dance with Hawk."

"Oh! I must confess I wasn't even thinking of that. I was thinking of Hawk. How short-sighted of me!"

Maddie gave an unladylike hoot of laughter. "And you imagine when Hawk is out there on the floor with his arms around you, he is thinking about anything as unromantic as guarding you?" She sighed in mock distress, then leaned closer.

"Hawk is thinking only about dancing with you, Caroline. I have never seen our sheriff so, um, shall I say inattentive to his duties."

Hawk strode across the room to claim Caroline again, a frown creasing his forehead and his dark eyebrows lowered.

In an instant Jericho was beside him. "Trouble?"

"Hell, yes, you smart-ass sharpshooter," he muttered under his breath. "Woman trouble."

Jericho glanced sideways at his wife, then slapped a friendly hand on Hawk's shoulder.

"Hell's half acre, Hawk, I never thought I'd see you flinch that way. You know, my friend, that woman trouble is the worst kind of trouble a man can have."

Chapter Twenty

I am worry for my lady. Here in this house of the sister of *Señor* Hawk she is safe, but I see in her face a true thing. She is worry too much.

All is kindness in this place, and my lady goes about freely. *Señor* Hawk has guards who are watch over her, but she is still fear something. Maybe she does not grow fond of this house because she knows to leave soon.

I have fear for this trap *Señor* Hawk is plan for sometime soon. If is a mistake, my lady will suffer.

Sunday morning after Jensen's barn dance, Caroline found herself alone in the kitchen with Ilsa. When Billy's mother had suggested he attend church with Eli, the old man's gray-speckled eyebrows had risen in surprise, but at a look from Ilsa, he had marched the grumbling boy out the front door just as the church bell began to toll.

Caroline stood at the stove stirring a kettle of strawberry jam. Ilsa's jam disappeared from the glass jelly dish faster than the fresh-churned three-pound blocks of butter purchased from the mercantile. Now the entire kitchen smelled heavenly, rich and fruity.

"Hawk has gone over to the sheriff's office," Ilsa said in answer to Caroline's unspoken question. "Sandy, his deputy, is a staunch Methodist—never misses a Sunday service."

Caroline nodded. Fernanda had just left for Mass at the Catholic Church. "Come, sit down," Ilsa invited. "I will pour you some coffee."

"I am not the least bit tired, Ilsa." She gave the jam a double figure-eight pass with the wooden spatula.

"Sit down anyway, Caroline. I want to tell you something."

"Oh? What about?"

"About Hawk."

Her stirring arm halted. "What is it? Has something happened?"

Ilsa purposefully set her mug down on the bleached muslin tablecloth. "It's about something that *did* happen, years ago. I want to tell you about it."

With an odd premonition, Caroline lifted the kettle off the heat and sank onto the straight-back chair opposite Hawk's older sister. "Tell me."

"It was years ago, when Hawk was a young man. I had married and left home by that time, but when this occurred, I came back to Butte City." Ilsa rose to fill Caroline's coffee mug.

"Hawk was married when he was just seventeen. Did you know that?"

Caroline tried to keep the surprise out of her voice. "No, I did not."

"To a young half-Spanish, half-Cherokee girl. Her name was Whitefern. She was quite beautiful. Our mother did not approve, but

Hawk married her anyway, and she came to live with them on the ranch." Ilsa hesitated.

Caroline sipped her coffee and waited.

"My stepfather, that is Hawk's father, didn't like Whitefern. Maybe it was because she was part Indian and he was half-Indian himself, so he disliked that part of himself because now he was Don Luis with the big ranchera and the beautiful English wife."

Caroline noticed that there was little coffee in Ilsa's mug. She started to rise. "Shall I fill your cup for you?"

"No. I need to finish this before Hawk returns."

A feeling of foreboding settled over Caroline like a shroud of black fog. Whatever it was, she knew instinctively that Hawk would not like Ilsa's telling her about it.

"Whitefern became pregnant and had a child. A boy. Don Luis was furious. He didn't want a part-Indian grandson inheriting the ranch someday, even though his own son was one-quarter Cherokee.

"One night there was a terrible argument at

the ranch house. Our mother sided with Hawk and Whitefern, but Don Luis would not listen. He sent Hawk into Butte City to bring a lawyer, and that night Whitefern took the baby and slipped off to return to her people in Mexico. Our mother went with her. Hawk knew nothing about it until…"

The hair on the back of Caroline's neck bristled. "Until?" She could scarcely voice the question because she didn't want to hear the answer.

Ilsa toyed with her mug of cold coffee, turning it around and around on the tablecloth until Caroline couldn't stand it one more minute. Gently she laid her hand over the older woman's work-worn one. "Tell me the rest."

Ilsa brushed her fingers across her eyes, then laid her hand in her lap. "There was an ambush. Somewhere out on the desert, on the way to the border, three men kidnapped Whitefern and the baby. And Momma. The next day…" Her voice choked off.

"The next day a neighboring rancher rode in and told Don Luis what he had found. Two women, one white, one part Mexican, had been raped and mutilated so badly they were almost unrecognizable. The baby's skull had been smashed in."

Caroline knew she was going to vomit. She dropped her head and concentrated on taking slow, deep breaths until the bile in her throat receded. "Go on."

"Don Luis sent a vaquero into town to find Hawk, and the two of them set out to bury the remains and track down the killers. Even then, Hawk could track better than anyone in the territory. But I wish he had never found what he found."

Caroline nodded in silence.

"On the way back to the ranch, someone shot Don Luis. He died before Hawk could get him home."

Ilsa paused and closed her eyes. "Hawk was never the same after that."

"Dear God in heaven," Caroline whispered.

"Hawk went to the Texas Rangers and told them he was going to hunt down the three men, and when he found them he was going to kill them. I remember he said they were going to die slowly. Hawk has enough Indian in him to know about such things. I never wanted to know what he meant.

"Anyway, he joined the Rangers so he wouldn't hang for murder because he was acting on his own. It took him almost a year, but he did find the men, and he did kill them. Because he wore a Texas Ranger star, he was held blameless. He was just nineteen years old."

Caroline swallowed hard and closed her eyes. "Ilsa, how did you find out about all this?"

"Hawk told me. When I came home to help at the ranch, he told me everything. I hated the place, especially after that, and Hawk was terrible to live with in those days. Later, Billy and I moved to Oregon, to Smoke River."

Ilsa's voice wavered, but it was Caroline who was sobbing. "Oh, Caroline, I should not have told you." The older woman touched her arm.

"Why did you?" Caroline said through her tears.

Ilsa fished a plain handkerchief from her skirt pocket and pressed it into her hand. "Because I thought you should know why I am now going to say something to you that is really none of my business."

Her heart dropped into her stomach. "What is it? Just say it."

"Don't hurt him, Caroline. I think my brother is beginning to care for you. Please, please, don't hurt him."

Fernanda watched Caroline scrubbing a pair of Billy's jeans over the metal washboard and shook her head. "*Mi corazón*, you are work too hard in this heat. Let me—"

"No." Caroline's voice sounded as if she had been weeping, and that was very strange. She ducked her head and continued to rub at a stubborn grass stain. Tears splashed down into the soapy wash water. "I need to do this."

"Ah," Fernanda sighed. "Then I will see more inside what needs to do." She pressed Caroline's shoulder, then moved through the back door into the kitchen.

Hawk sat at the table, hunched over a mug of coffee.

"*Señor*," Fernanda said softly. "Do you know why my lady scrub at washboard and weep?"

Hawk's head jerked up. "No. Why is she?"

"Which, why she scrub? Or why she weep?"

"Weep, of course." With one boot he kicked a chair out for the Mexican woman to sit down. When she did, he reached over and touched her hand. "I dunno why she's crying, Fernanda. We haven't had words, and I haven't done anything dumb. At least I don't think I have."

"What does 'have words' mean? We, now, are 'have words,' no?"

Hawk grinned at her. "'Have words' means to have *bad* words. Like an argument."

Fernanda nodded. "Caroline is good girl. She has never like 'bad words.' Maybe she is too, how you say, soft?"

"She's soft, all right. Sure as shootin', she's all woman."

Fernanda sat up straight. "And you, *señor*? You are 'all man' as I hear it is said?"

He stared at her. "That's a mighty odd question. What is it you really want to know?"

"*Señor*, I know something of men. Once in Mexico I was much courted, so I know of men."

"Yeah? What do you know?" Hawk always liked talking with Fernanda; she usually had something worth saying. He was beginning to like this conversation even better because it was about Caroline.

"I know, *señor*, that men desire women."

"Hell, that's not new. Ever since Adam and Eve—"

Fernanda looked straight into his eyes without the usual twinkle in her shiny black depths. "And I know that sometimes is only that a man has itch and he wants to scratch it. *Comprende*?"

Hawk said nothing. Did Fernanda think he—

Hell, yes, she did think that. And she thought that because he *did* have an itch, an overwhelming, aching itch, he damn well wanted to scratch it.

He met the Mexican woman's steady gaze. Fernanda was telling him something in addition: do not scratch his itch with Caroline.

Chapter Twenty-One

"Fishing?" Caroline stopped stirring the bubbling kettle of applesauce and stared at Hawk's nephew. "Thank you, Billy, but I don't think—"

"Aw, c'mon, Miss Caroline. I bet you never been fishing back in Boston. Bet you don't know how to bait a hook or nothin'."

She wiped the perspiration from her forehead and smiled at the boy. "No, I can't say that I do."

"You don't know what you're missing," Billy insisted. He jiggled a metal bucket in front of her. "Worms," he explained.

She risked a peek and wished she hadn't. A mass of pink crawly things writhed at the bottom of Billy's pail. The thought of touching the wriggly things turned her stomach.

"Please," Billy begged. "Mama packed a picnic basket. Besides, you can't make apple-sauce all day."

Ilsa turned away from the bowl of apples she was peeling. "Oh, go on, Caroline. This batch is almost done. Fernanda can help me fill the jars."

"Oh, no, Ilsa, I—"

Fernanda made shooing motions with her hands. "Go, *hija.* You are, how you say, under the foot!"

Billy tugged at her gingham apron. "The river's only a couple of miles from town, an' it's real pretty. Uncle Hawk won't mind."

That decided the matter. She needed some time away from the tall, blunt-spoken sheriff of Smoke River. Not only was he at her side almost every hour of every day, he was beginning to invade her dreams, as well.

She was seeing another side to Hawk Rivera, one she would never have suspected from the first eight days she had known him. Here in Smoke River, where he wasn't on constant alert every minute of the day and night, she was learning that Hawk could be lighthearted and jovial as at the dance, even playful. She hated to admit it, but she liked his teasing, even when it concerned her underclothes.

She liked dancing with him, too, being close to him and feeling his arms around her. No man had ever breached the defenses she had erected after her father had ruined her.

"Billy," Ilsa said. "I put a jar of lemonade in your lunch basket. When it's empty, bring home some blackberries in it."

"Miss Caroline, are ya comin' or not?" Billy demanded.

"Well, I suppose…yes, all right, Billy. You can teach me how to fish."

Billy grabbed his pole and the bait bucket and bolted for the front door and Caroline reached behind her to untie her apron. At that moment the screen door wheezed open.

"Whoa," Hawk said. "Where are you off to in such a hurry?"

"Miss Caroline and I are goin' fishing!"

Hawk shot a look at her and his dark eyebrows rose. "You are, are you?"

She caught her breath at his expression. "Yes, I thought—"

"No, you're not." His voice was quiet but there was no mistaking his intent. "Not unless I come along."

"Sure, Uncle Hawk. I got plenty of hooks."

Over his shoulder Caroline saw Ilsa and Fernanda exchange a look. Ilsa's lips thinned. Fernanda just threw up her hands and shook her head, but Ilsa kept studying the paring knife in her hand. "Don't be late for supper."

"Hurry up, Uncle Hawk. The fish'll be sleeping by the time we get to the river."

Hawk snatched the picnic basket off the kitchen table. "All right, let's go wake 'em up."

They tramped an hour and a half through the woods before they reached the river, clear and gently flowing except where the blue-green water rippled over half-submerged boulders. As usual, Hawk carried his rifle, and his Colt was strapped to his hip.

The sun was hot, but it was cool and pleasant under the canopy of willow and vine maple trees along the bank. Billy dumped half the worms and three hooks out onto the grass for Hawk and Caroline, then disappeared around a bend.

Caroline averted her eyes from the crawling mess, but Hawk stood his rifle against a tree trunk, slid his jackknife out of his jeans pocket, and cut two thin branches for fishing poles. He tied a length of string onto the ends and attached the other end to a hook, then speared a worm and handed the pole to Caroline.

"What d-do I do with it?" she sputtered.

"Fish," he said drily. "Like this." He baited his own hook and swung it out over the water, where it landed with a soft plop.

Caroline tossed her hook out and waited. After a few minutes she decided her line wasn't reaching far enough, so she yanked it in, took a step toward the river bank and flung it out again. Still not far enough. She pulled it in once more and tossed it out even farther. Then she leaned forward to watch it land and she lost her balance. With a cry she splashed into the water.

Hawk dropped his pole and strode into the chest-deep river, grabbed the waistband of her skirt and hauled her upright. Water streamed off her face, and her shirtwaist and skirt were plastered to her body.

He reached to steady her, but she grabbed onto his forearm and unbalanced him. The next thing he knew he tipped sideways and they both tumbled into the river. He managed to regain his footing and grasped Caroline's shoulders. They both struggled up the bank and onto dry ground.

"Hey," Billy called. "You guys okay?"

"We're fine," Hawk shouted. "Wet, but fine," he added quietly. Water sluiced off his chest and his jeans, and his holster and revolver were soaked. To his surprise, Caroline was laughing.

He helped her over to a thick patch of camas grass. "Stretch out here in the sun and let your clothes dry out." He unstrapped his gun belt, sat down beside her and began to wipe down the Colt using the gingham tablecloth Ilsa had packed in the picnic basket.

"I don't think I like fishing," Caroline said. "It's dangerous. We could drown."

Hawk had to laugh. "You ladies from Boston never fall in rivers, huh?"

"Never." She spread out her skirt and folded her hands over her midriff. "How long will it take for me to dry out?"

"About half an hour. But…"

She gazed up at him. "But?" Her dark lashes were wet, he noted. Made her eyes look bigger and bluer. Her hair had come loose from the twist at her neck and it now fell to her shoulders in soft waves.

"But," he continued with a chuckle, "if you want your underwear to dry, it'll take longer. Of course you could just leave them kinda wet and squishy if you'd rather."

"How much longer?"

"Maybe an hour." He checked the chambers on his revolver and shook out the water, reloaded it and laid it aside. Then he stretched out beside her in the hot sunshine and closed his eyes.

All it took was five minutes lying next to her, smelling the lemony-rose fragrance of her hair, before he decided this was going to be the longest hour in his life. He glanced sideways at her.

Her eyes were closed, so he felt free to watch her breasts rise and fall with her breathing. He liked that. Even better, her nipples showed where the wet fabric of her shirtwaist clung.

He forced his gaze away, studied the trees growing along the bank, the huckleberry bushes, the flat-topped boulder in the shallow part of the river—anything to keep from looking at her.

Yeah, you've got one hell of an itch, and an overwhelming urge to scratch it. He ached with it. But Fernanda was right; he couldn't scratch it with Caroline.

Damnation. She was the only woman he'd felt anything for since the long-ago marriage of his youth. He'd thought his scars were so deep he'd never feel anything again, but here it was, plain as warts on a frog. Caroline Mac-Farlane made him feel alive again. Made him feel that maybe life might be worth living after all.

He glanced again at her face, her wet wavy hair, her small delicate hands folded primly on her stomach and felt an unfamiliar lurch inside his chest. He wanted to hold her. Continue to keep her safe.

The realization stopped his heartbeat. This was more than an itch. More than wanting her. Much more. What he wanted was more than he could ask of a woman who had her own scars and was determined to keep on traveling around the country and making speeches to avoid them. He had absolutely no place in her life.

"Hawk?" Her voice sounded drowsy. "What is it? I can hear you thinking."

"Yeah? How can you tell?"

"Your breathing is getting jerky. Is it about the trap you plan to set?"

He snorted a laugh. "In a way, I guess."

"Are you getting dry? Your clothes, I mean?"

Hell, no, he wasn't getting dry. He was getting wet and hard and desperate. He couldn't go on like this much longer.

"Sure, I'm getting dry."

She sat up suddenly and leaned over him. "You're lying." Her hair brushed his face and he opened his mouth to catch a strand. It tasted of rosewater, he guessed. Something sweet and a little spicy.

"I have an idea," she announced.

"Oh, yeah? I'm listening."

"First we tell the newspapers that I'm going to give a speech about women and the vote. Then we ask them to wire other newspapers in the state to spread the word. That sh-should attract whoever it is who hates me enough to want me dead, don't you think?"

He looked up at her. She was so animated by the plan it sent a pain into his gut. "No."

"Why not? Don't you think it's a good idea?"

He groaned. He didn't want to think about a plan or a trap or anything else but her. "It's a good plan, Caroline. But right about now I don't want to think about it."

He curved one hand around her neck and pulled her down so her mouth brushed his. At the first touch of her lips he reached his other hand to her head, laced his fingers in her still-damp hair, and made it a real kiss.

She didn't pull back, and that surprised him. Without breaking contact he half sat up and went on kissing her, deepening it until his blood thrummed in his ears and he felt like he was going to explode.

With his thumb he gently touched the hollow of her throat. Her pulse was racing and her breathing grew uneven as his kiss stretched on and on.

Damn, what was happening?

He lifted his mouth away from hers and relaxed his hand, but she didn't jerk away as he expected. Instead she brought her fingers to lightly graze his cheek.

"What are we doing?" she said, her voice shaky.

"Damned if I know." He thought a minute. "Fernanda told me..."

"And Ilsa said things, also."

"Do you want me to stop?"

"No," she breathed. "I do not."

He reached for her again just as Billy's voice rang out. "I caught ten fish!" The boy trotted around the bend, his face flushed with success. "Uncle Hawk, can we eat 'em for supper?"

Hawk blew out a long breath, sat upright and drew apart from Caroline. "Sure, Billy. You clean 'em, and we'll eat 'em."

"Uncle Hawk, I'm hungry! Let's eat lunch."

"Yeah," Hawk said quietly. "I'm hungry, too. Guess lunch will have to do," he murmured.

Without a word Caroline unpacked the wicker basket and handed out four chicken sandwiches. "There is a bowl of potato salad but only two forks, so we will have to share." Her voice shook slightly and her lips tingled from Hawk's kiss.

She wondered at herself, ignoring Ilsa's warning so blatantly. Ever since Ilsa told her about the tragic death of Hawk's family, she couldn't look at him without wondering how he had survived. Did he have nightmares, too?

Did he relive the awful parts about what had happened over and over in his mind, as she did?

No wonder he could be brutally direct at times. It was a miracle he could even smile.

She would not hurt Hawk, she resolved. He was showing her something about herself, helping her heal, helping her conquer her fear of men. In exchange she would give him something that he needed, something she wanted to give him. He was healing her scars; maybe she could heal his.

The three of them devoured the contents of the picnic basket, right down to Eli's sugar cookies and the jar of lemonade, which they passed back and forth.

"You catch anything, Uncle Hawk?"

Hawk chuckled and ruffled his nephew's russet hair. "You ask too many questions."

Billy paused, a cookie halfway to his mouth. "Huh?"

Caroline smiled at the boy. "Your uncle means he will answer you when he has something to say."

"You guys are sure weird today," Billy observed. "You haven't caught any fish and you're both all wet, and... Oh, well, all grown-ups are a little strange, I guess."

He grabbed the fishing pole he'd laid beside the picnic basket and marched off to the edge of the river. "I can see the trout even from here!" he yelled. "Guess you just didn't know how to catch 'em, huh, Uncle Hawk?"

"Guess so," Hawk called. He caught Caroline's eyes and held them until she thought she would melt from the heat in his gaze.

He touched her arm. "I can't sit here close to you with Billy ten yards away."

Caroline nodded. "Let's look for blackberries," she suggested. "Ilsa told Billy to bring some back."

"Yeah," he said, his voice rough. "Maybe if I keep busy, I can keep my hands off you."

Maybe.

Hours later, when they returned to the house, Ilsa marveled at the lemonade jar and the picnic basket overflowing with ripe blackberries. "And twelve big trout. My, you all have been busy."

Caroline was afraid to look at Hawk, afraid Ilsa would see her kiss-swollen lips. Fernanda took one look at her and simply folded her into an embrace.

"You have sunburn, *mi corazón*. And your hair it flies away. I will fix."

Chapter Twenty-Two

The Smoke River summer *chautauqua* fell on the following Sunday. Caroline had never heard of a *Chautauqua,* in Boston they held summer concerts and operettas in the park, and sometimes a troupe of actors performed one of Shakespeare's comedies. But she had to admit she was curious about what a little town like Smoke River could produce in the way of entertainment.

It had been a blistering hot day, the kind that kept her camisole damp with perspiration and made her long to lift up her skirt and petticoat to let the air cool her legs. By evening, the entire town had collected at the tiny tree-studded park to sit on the grass and drink lemonade or smoke pipes and slap at the occasional mosquito.

Seated on a blanket in the shade between Hawk and Billy, Caroline fanned herself with one of the pleated squares of paper Fernanda had fashioned into fans for Ilsa and herself.

"Sure is hot," Billy complained, tugging at the tight collar of his best Sunday shirt. Caroline offered her fan, but he pushed her hand away. "Fannin' my face like that'd make me look like a sissy or an old lady."

Caroline smiled. "Do you think I am a sissy or an old lady? Or Fernanda or your mother?"

"Naw. Girls are already sissies."

She laughed. "We are, are we? What makes us sissies?"

Billy's rust-colored eyebrows drew into a frown. "'Cuz girls don't like to get dirty or pick up worms or clean fish guts."

Caroline flinched at the word *guts* and heard Hawk's chuckle. "You are quite right about worms and fish…um…entrails." There was an element of truth to Billy's philosophy; however, she wanted to point out that girls were also good at things like public speaking, and writing, and music. "Girls are good at many other things, Billy, such as playing hopscotch and baking pies and knitting scarves."

"But—"

"And thinking fast on their feet," Hawk interjected.

"But—"

"Let it go, Billy," Hawk said.

"And," Ilsa said with a severe look over her shoulder at her son, "let's not spoil this lovely summer evening with quarreling. Do I make myself clear?"

"Aw, Ma…"

While Billy wrangled with his mother, Caroline studied the surroundings. A wooden stage had been erected on the lush grass, with a theater curtain that looked suspiciously like four quilted bedspreads gathered onto a pole. Kerosene lamps arrayed at the front of the platform provided footlights of a sort, and Carl Ness, acting as a master of ceremonies, welcomed the crowd to the festivities.

"Tonight, the citizens of Smoke River present our third annual summer musicale, and the show will include the fine talents of town folk you all know." He retired to a spattering of applause, and the quilt curtain opened to reveal four men, all dressed in red shirts and blue suspenders.

"Why," Ilsa exclaimed, "there's the barber, Whitey Poletti. I didn't know he could sing."

Hawk leaned close to Caroline and spoke in her ear. "Hope he can sing better than he can cut hair."

The quartet launched into "Home, Sweet Home." Whitey Poletti's rich, honey-sweet tenor soared over the rapt listeners, and Caroline sent Hawk an *I-told-you-so* look.

"He's Italian," he intoned.

Thunderous applause greeted each of the quartet's songs, and finally after two encores, the curtain was pulled closed. Hawk subtly positioned himself so his shoulder touched Caroline's, then bent his head to whisper near her ear.

"Remember your idea for laying my trap?"

Her heart began to pound. "Will it be soon? I am getting jittery just thinking about it."

"Soon enough. Tomorrow I'll contact both newspapers in town to spread the word."

She sucked in her breath. She was frightened. Even more than that, Hawk's nearness, and the soap and bay rum scent of his skin, was sending shivers up her spine.

"What's wrong?" he murmured.

"N-nothing, I guess."

"Want to change your mind?"

"No. I know the feeling of safety I have here cannot last. I must move forward."

"Damn," he breathed. He increased the pressure of his shoulder against hers. "Kinda figured as much."

The curtain parted again and a small figure in a starched pink pinafore stood alone on the stage. Billy jerked upright, his brown eyes riveted on the girl.

"Manette Nicolet," Hawk breathed. Eli reached out a bony hand and poked Billy in the ribs.

Manette looked like a small, dainty angel

with pink ribbons in her blonde hair. She waited until quiet descended over the audience, and then she began to sing.

"Au clare de la lune, mon ami Pierrot..."

Her voice was exquisite, a clear, high soprano that brought tears to Caroline's eyes. Billy sat with his mouth hanging open until the end of the third verse, and when the crowd erupted into cheers and clapping, the boy looked as if he'd been poleaxed.

"He's in love," Hawk muttered. "Poor kid." He hadn't meant for Caroline to overhear and her response surprised him.

"He is not 'poor.' He is fortunate."

He blinked at that. "Thought you didn't think much of love," he said quietly.

"I—"

The curtain jerked open once more, and now the little stage was crowded with musicians—Thad MacAllister playing the fiddle, along with a banjo player and someone plucking away on the washtub bass Caroline had wondered about at last Saturday's barn dance. They roared through "Turkey in the Straw" and "Camptown Races," trying to outdo each other with runs and flourishes and little unexpected turns.

"You ever hear music like this?" Hawk whispered.

"Never."

He leaned closer. "Makes me want to kiss you."

She gasped. "What?"

"I said—"

"I heard what you said," she whispered. "Why on earth would all this noise make you want—?"

"Hell's bells," he murmured, "I want to kiss you even when it's quiet."

"Hawk! Do stop."

"Can't. Been thinking about it ever since we sat down."

"Hush. We are in view of everyone in town."

"Yeah. That's why I'm not kissing you."

She pulled sideways to stare at him. "We were discussing our plan to flush out…"

Hawk gave a soft groan. A large part of him wanted to stop everything right here, tonight, and not move forward with anything except being close to her. Another part of him knew it had to be done. Otherwise, Caroline would never know a moment of peace.

Suddenly she stiffened. "Hawk, look." She tipped her head toward a knot of men standing on the sidelines. He followed her gaze, then checked to make sure Rooney Cloudman and Marshal Johnson were in position. He recognized all the men in the knot except for two; one was young and green-looking, in a spiffed-up shirt and shiny new boots. The other man was Overby.

Overby? What was he doing here?

Hawk caught Rooney's eye and pointed. Rooney sent him a grin that made Hawk feel like an overprotective mother hen. Quietly he slipped his arm around Caroline's waist and pulled her closer.

"Don't worry. Rooney and the marshal have them covered." He kept his arm in place.

Caroline turned toward him and her chin brushed his shoulder. "I want this whole thing to be over with."

"Me, too. It will be. Just need a few more days, enough time for the newspapers to spread the word."

"How many days?"

"Three, maybe four."

She sighed out a shaky breath. "I don't know if I can stand waiting."

"You can stand it," he said softly. "I've seen you under pressure. You don't buckle."

"I feel like it, though."

"We're gonna get him, Caroline. Whoever it is, we'll get him."

If the man stalking her turned out to be Overby, he was as good as got right this instant. He curved his hand around her rib cage and kept it there, relishing the warmth of her body under the lacy shirtwaist, feeling her breath pull in and out. Caroline was alive and responsive and he wanted to be a lot closer than he was.

Yeah, but what the hell are you going to do about her afterward? The minute they caught their man, she'd be leaving to continue her speaking tour. He didn't want to let her go, but he knew he couldn't keep her, either. But Lord knew he couldn't take much more of this in-between stuff.

The next musicale acts went on but Hawk couldn't concentrate. He tried thinking about anything other than the woman beside him, but his mind was a muddle.

The last presentation was a real surprise. The curtain parted and there stood Verena Forester, dressed in a sober black dress with a black lace shawl about her narrow shoulders. But her face, my God. Her face was luminous with emotion.

She raised one arm and started to recite something—poetry, he guessed from the lilt of the lines. The audience hung on every word. Her voice was low and musical, full of real depth of feeling. Hawk stared at the woman, wondering why he'd never thought of her as anything but a dried-up old maid dressmaker.

The poem was about love and loss.

"And over the waves, and over the seas, she searched for her lover. Through wind and through storm, through gales and through rain…

But she never will find him again…"

By the time Verena was halfway through her recitation, Caroline was in tears, along with Ilsa and Fernanda and most of the women in the listening crowd. Hawk himself had an unexpectedly thick throat.

They walked home in silence, Billy still starry-eyed, Eli surreptitiously wiping his cheeks with his bandanna, and Ilsa and Fernanda close together with their arms linked.

Hawk and Caroline moved in step with each other along the quiet street, not speaking and not touching. He could tell she was intensely aware of him beside her; tonight he was more aware than he had ever been of the current between them, how it danced along his veins and spoke to her. Invited her. God, what was he thinking? *Not with Caroline.*

He wanted her so much he was blind with it. *Not with Caroline.*

When they reached the house, he stopped

her with a hand on her arm. "Walk around the block with me."

"Why?"

"Just once. Let the others all go up to bed."

She nodded, and they turned back down the street.

It was the longest block he could ever remember. When they returned to the porch steps, the house was dark except for a single small lamp on the table near the stairs.

Caroline headed for the staircase, but again he stopped her. "Wait." He leaned forward and blew out the flame. Then he took her hand and led her up the steps.

Outside her bedroom door he drew her to a halt, placed his hands on her shoulders and turned her away from him. Then he stepped in close and began to remove the hairpins securing the twist at the back of her neck. Her breath caught, but she didn't move. He collected each wire pin and slid them into his shirt pocket.

He gathered her hair in both his hands and lifted it to expose her bare neck, then bent and pressed his mouth against her skin. She smelled of vanilla and she tasted, oh, God, she tasted like roses.

"Caroline."

She tipped her head forward and he kissed her again.

"Caroline, come to bed with me. Now. Tonight. Before this plan of ours is put in motion and time gets away from us."

A long, pregnant silence fell, and then she turned to face him, a question in her eyes.

Chapter Twenty-Three

"Hawk? I am frightened of… Well, you know that, do you not?"

"I know," he said, his voice quiet. "Let me show you what it can be like." He wrapped his arm about her shoulder and walked her past her bedroom door, on down to the very end of the hallway.

His door opened onto a sparsely furnished room, with a chest of drawers on one wall, a plain table that served as a desk, now piled with books and writing papers, and one tall paned window. His bed stood beneath it, and Caroline saw that it was positioned so that from a prone position he could see out into the tree branches. A sturdy-looking bookcase served as a nightstand.

At her questioning look he gestured at the desk. "I read some at night."

"Oh? What sort of things?"

He moved to the window, released the catch and raised it as high as it would go. A rush of cool, sweet-smelling air flowed in.

"History, mostly. Some Dickens."

She hid her surprise, then remembered that his mother had been English and that he had tutors when he was young. Hawk was unusual to say the least. A Texas Ranger sheriff who read Dickens.

A man who wanted to make love to her.

Her breath caught. *Could she?* She wanted him to, but… Could she?

Outside two song sparrows twittered and chirruped in the tree branches. In the half dark of this late-summer evening there was no other sound but their breathing.

Hawk moved toward her, stopping to face her without speaking. Very deliberately he lifted his hands to her shoulders and just stood there, waiting.

"I figured you might not want this after you

thought about it. Do you?" His voice sounded slightly hoarse.

"Yes," she whispered. "And no."

"Hell, Caroline, tell me now, before I make a damn fool of myself."

She reached to touch his chest. Under her palm his heartbeat was erratic. "I will tell you after you kiss me," she said. "Oh, Lord, what a brazen thing to say! Somehow when I am around you I feel…unexpected things."

"Yeah?" He placed his thumb under her chin and tipped her face up to his. "Like what?" His lips came to rest against her forehead. "Tell me."

She couldn't look at him so she closed her eyes. "Well, I feel…happy."

He brushed his mouth over her eyelids, then moved to a spot just behind her left ear and flicked his tongue against her skin. A dart of pleasure pricked, and she hissed in a breath.

"Oh," she murmured. She angled her head to give him better access and felt his tongue circle lazily into the shell of her ear.

This time the jolt of sensation went all the

way to her belly and below. It was astonishing how much she liked the feeling.

"Hawk," she murmured. "You haven't kissed me yet."

He gave a soft laugh. "I was hoping you'd notice that." He pressed slow, feathery kisses under her ear, across her cheek, on the underside of her jaw. His lips were warm against her skin, and when the sound of his breathing grew ragged, another thrill shot through her. All at once she realized she held a kind of power over him. It made her feel safe. Not helpless, but in control somehow.

At last his mouth settled on hers and began to move over her lips, gently at first and then more urgently. When he lifted his head she was trembling.

He kissed her again, deepened it and made a low noise in his throat. Without breaking contact he lifted her hand to his neck, and when she brought her other hand to join it, he made that noise again.

"Caroline," he said against her mouth. "Do you like this?"

"Yes," she whispered. "Don't stop."

He laughed gently. "Trust me, if this is what you want, I won't."

She felt his fingers rest on the top button of her shirtwaist and then carefully slip it free and move to the next, and the next.

"So many damn buttons," he said near her ear. His voice sounded raspy. He lifted the lacy fabric away and put his mouth on her bare skin.

"Glad you gave up wearing a corset," he murmured. His warm breath washed over her chest and he kissed and unbuttoned until the garment was open to her waist; he tugged it free of her waistband and let it flutter to the floor. Then he untied the ribbon at the neck of her camisole and it, too, drifted to the floor.

His warm hand cupped her breast and she felt a stab of pleasure all the way to her toes. Before she could draw breath, he dipped his head and licked her nipple, and she made a sound she had never made in her entire life.

The next thing she knew his mouth covered the tip and she thought she would die of pleasure. Such a small thing, his tongue swirling against her flesh, but it was an exquisite thing. *Exquisite.* She never wanted him to stop, wanted him to go on forever laving her flesh with his tongue.

He lifted his head and looked into her eyes. "Do you want this?" he asked softly. "Because if you don't, you'd better stop me now."

It was the first time she had ever heard Hawk's voice sound hesitant. "I do want this. I want…you."

He unbuttoned his shirt, shrugged out of it and tossed it behind him without looking. She heard his gun belt thud onto the floor, and then he was unsnapping her skirt and untying her petticoat and pushing them down off her hips. He rested his hand on the elastic of her pantalets, tugged once and slid them off.

Using both hands he touched her all over, smoothing his fingers over every inch of her exposed skin and following with his mouth and his tongue. His tongue, especially, did something extraordinary to her insides. Something addictive. She began to swell in places she'd never paid attention to, and in those same places she ached in ways she had never dreamed of.

Something was happening to her, something that was wonderful and scary and exquisitely pleasurable.

He lifted her into his arms, moved forward and laid her on his bed. She watched him shuck his boots, unbutton his jeans and strip them off, along with his drawers and his socks. When he was naked, he sat down beside her on the bed and took her hand.

"You can still back out," he whispered.

In answer she grasped his hand and tugged him down to lie beside her.

Hawk was careful not to press his body against hers at first; instead, he used his hands, running his palms over her belly, her breasts, and then moving to her inner thighs. Finally he let his fingers rest on her mound of dark curls.

She lay very still, and he wondered if he'd gone too far, too fast. But she pressed her own hand over his and he felt like he'd been released from prison. Gently he slid his fore-finger into her soft, damp folds and when she sucked air in between her teeth he smiled into the dark. She was wet and hot and so beautiful he wanted to weep.

Imagine that, he thought. He, Anderson Rivera. Hawk, as he'd become known, the scourge of the Mescalero Apache, weeping at the feel of a woman under his hand. *This was sure as hell a first for him.*

But damnation, that's just what he felt like doing.

She moaned and moved her hips subtly, and he slipped his finger all the way inside her and held his breath. When her small hand tenta-tively touched his manhood, he about came up off the bed.

"That feels good!"

"Does it really?"

He couldn't answer, just silently begged her not to stop. She moved her fingers over his throbbing flesh and he thought he would die and float up to heaven.

Was she ready for him?

He moved his finger inside her, then slid it out and sought the nub above her entrance. When he found it, her uneven breath told him all he needed to know. He stroked and circled while she slowly, so slowly touched his member with her soft, warm hand and he closed his eyes in ecstasy.

God, it had never been like this before. Never.

She began to move with him as he touched her and all at once he realized he was too close. He lifted her hand away from him, then stroked his finger inside her and leaned over to kiss her. Her arms came around him, pulling him closer. Pulling him on top of her.

He rose over her and positioned himself at her entrance. He couldn't stop now; he prayed she would come with him.

He entered her gradually, a little at a time, watching her face. "Caroline, look into my eyes."

Holding her gaze, he thrust into her as gently as he could and waited, his heart hammering. God, she was small and so tight he wondered if she…

She looked up at him and—*goddamn*—she was smiling! Oh, yes. Yes!

He withdrew partway and thrust again, and again, moving steadily, deliberately, and when she lifted her hips to meet him he was lost. He heard her cry out, but it wasn't in fear, it was something else.

A rush of possessiveness and tenderness and pride all mixed up together pulsed through him, and he began to move with more purpose. Just when he sensed his release was coming, she cried out again and called his name, and that pushed him over the edge.

When he came back to himself he was still lying on top of her and she was looking at him with the oddest expression in her eyes.

"Caroline? Are you all right? Did I hurt you?"

"Oh, Hawk, at this moment I am more 'all right' than I have ever been in my life." She raised her head to kiss him and his heart damn near stopped. Tears glistened on her cheeks.

"Caroline?"

She sent him a slow, languorous smile. "Do

not be concerned, Hawk. I always cry when I'm happy."

His own eyes stung. He blinked hard and kissed her damp eyelids.

Chapter Twenty-Four

Hawk awoke at dawn to find Caroline propped up on one elbow, staring down at him. Outside the window, the sky was just shading from gray into peach; inside his bedroom it felt like it was all sunshine.

"You were asleep," she observed. There was a warmth in her voice that hadn't been there yesterday; he prayed he had something to do with it. In fact, he wanted *everything* to do with it.

"Until a minute ago, yeah." He crooked his arm about her neck and pulled her mouth down to his. A sweeter woman he had never tasted. When he released her she settled back onto the pillow with a sigh.

"I have to go," he said.

"Where? The sheriff's office again? Does poor Sandy ever get to arrest anyone?" she asked with a soft laugh.

He sat up, pulled her into his arms and buried his face in the tangle of dark hair tumbling down her bare back. It smelled like honeysuckle. And a little like him, he imagined.

"I'm going to relieve Sandy, yes. Then I'll stop by the *Lark* and the *Sentinel* offices to set this trap operation in motion."

"Oh, Hawk, don't you sometimes wish that time could stop? For a while, anyway?"

"You mean so we could have all morning to make love? Yeah, I do wish that."

"It's a good thing neither of us is lord of the universe, then. Otherwise, crops all over Oregon would fry in the sun."

He chuckled quietly. "I'd sacrifice a few thousand acres of wheat to get another hour with you."

"Ranchers would hate you."

"Would you?" He waited, wanting to hear something sweet and irrational from her lips.

"No, I would not hate you, Hawk. Another hour with you might be well worth thousands of bushels of burned wheat. At least for me."

With a groan he rolled out of bed, pulled on his drawers and his jeans, and buckled his Colt around his hips. She watched him button his shirt and splash water from the pitcher onto his face. He'd shave later. Probably slice his chin to ribbons with her looking at him and his hand shaking like it was.

He glanced over to where she lay half-covered by the sheet. God and little fishes, she was beautiful. Had he told her that last night? Probably not. There was a whole lot he'd wanted to say, but his brain hadn't been too clear last night. He would say them another night.

If they ever had another night.

He bent to kiss her, then straightened and headed for the door. He couldn't look at her again or he'd never make it out of the house.

At the foot of the stairs he met Fernanda. Hands on her ample hips, her face unsmiling, the Mexican woman looked him right in the eye and slowly shook her head.

Hawk took her shoulders and planted a smacking kiss on each of her cheeks. "Take her some coffee, will you, Fernanda? She's had a…long night."

He was out the door before she could swear at him in Spanish.

Fernanda watched the tall *gringo* sheriff stride down the porch steps and set off up the street. First she scowled, and then she blew out a long, long breath, and then a smile began to curve her lips.

"*Si, señor.* Coffee," she murmured. She touched her fingers to her cheek and turned into the kitchen.

Hawk paid a visit to the *Lake County Lark*, where he spoke with the editor, Cole Sanders, then went across the street to Jessamine Lassiter's *Sentinel* office. He fed the same details to each publisher and was assured that both newspapers would run the announcement and an accompanying feature story about Caroline MacFarlane within a day of each other.

He took no joy in the enthusiasm of both publishers. As a matter of honest fact he felt as if a heavy black net of four-ply rope had been dropped over him.

By Tuesday, when the *Lark* was published, Hawk started to hear snatches of excited talk from the townspeople. By Wednesday, Cole Sanders assured him, word had spread to the surrounding counties, and by Thursday the telegraph operator at the railway station would be alerting the entire state of Oregon and beyond.

Caroline's speech was set for Saturday afternoon, and it was all Hawk could think about. Now, at the sheriff's office, he slammed his desk drawer shut so hard the glass of bourbon Mayor Harvey O'Grady was sharing with him teetered dangerously near the edge. Harvey reached out and steadied the half-full tumbler.

"Son," he began.

Hawk hated it when the mayor used that term. He hadn't been anybody's son since he was eighteen years old, but Harvey had lost his firstborn at Antietam, so Hawk never objected.

"You're jumpier than a grasshopper on a griddle," the mayor observed.

"Sorry, Harve. Guess I am, a bit."

Harvey peered at him over the rim of his steel spectacles and pursed his lips. "Just so's you know, boyo, I'm backin' you up. Along with Sandy and Jericho and ever'body else you got lined up."

"Thanks, Harve."

"She means somethin' to you, does she?"

Hawk combed the fingers of one hand through his overlong hair. "Yeah. Don't know how it happened. Wish it hadn't." That was an out-and-out lie, but Harvey probably saw through it. Hawk gulped down another swallow of bourbon.

"Hawk," the older man said. "You're lyin'. Now, I don't care if you're lyin', but *she* might. So watch what you say from here on out."

Harvey heaved himself to his feet and went through the sheriff's office door, and Hawk sat without moving for a good quarter hour. He had some things to say to her all right. But it wouldn't be until this business was over and they could both start to sleep nights.

People began streaming into Smoke River, women bearing hand-lettered signs, men with grim faces who hung out in the Golden Partridge and tried to drown what they saw coming in booze and tinny piano music. Jingo's stagecoach business increased fourfold, and every time the grizzled older man passed Hawk entering or leaving town, he saluted and sent him a toothy grin and a thumbs-up. The hotels in both Smoke River and Gillette Springs were filled to bursting, and both newspaper offices were flooded with letters to the editor. Cole Sanders confided that he'd be glad when the whole thing was over.

Hawk felt split right down the middle, half anxious for the conclusion of his plan and half dreading what it would mean when it was finally finished and Caroline would resume her travels and speech-making.

He couldn't think about it now. He had to think about every detail of the operation, right down to how many people could crowd into the meeting hall behind the barbershop and where they'd be sitting and which of his friends would be positioned where.

In the back of his mind he knew he was more frightened than he'd ever been in his life, even when chasing three murdering renegades into Mexico. This morning he found he couldn't relax long enough to sit at Ilsa's kitchen table while she and Fernanda scrambled eggs and flipped pancakes.

By afternoon he found himself pacing around the backyard where Caroline was hanging up wet shirts and jeans with Billy beside her, handing her clothespins. He chopped a mountain of wood just to give himself something to do, and he tried like hell to keep his eyes off her slim form when she stretched her arms up to the clothesline.

Twice his ax glanced off a chunk of oak, and that's when he knew he was in trouble. Tomorrow afternoon he would need every scrap of concentration he could muster.

Caroline stopped suddenly and sent him a

look across the woodpile that made his heart stop. He blew out a long breath and wiped the sweat off his forehead with his shirtsleeve. Tomorrow should go like clockwork.

It had to. It was a simple matter of life and death.

Chapter Twenty-Five

I am worry too much. Is each day I do
this and I do not stop, so I go often to the
white church and ask Holy Mary to protect my lady. And *Señor* Hawk.

I fear for her tomorrow, when this thing
will happen. I also fear for him, but it is
not because of men and guns and what
will be. I fear for him because I know in
this house who sleep where.

My lady she is look different. She has
smile and long times with no speaking, and
she sing when she cook breakfast and when
she wash clothes and when she go up the
stairs at night. *Madre mia*, I ask you, watch
over your children and keep them safe.

I think tomorrow will be very hard. I
know *Señor* Hawk he is a good man, so
I ask please God to keep safe so my lady
she can go on with singing.

Caroline dressed with extra care in the forest
green poplin skirt with the flounces Hawk had
insisted on and a plain white shirtwaist with
a ruffle at her wrist deep enough to hide the
shaking of her hands.

Hawk had risen while it was still dark outside, kissed her with restrained urgency and
silently left the room. She listened through the
open window for the sharp sound of his boot
heels but heard nothing. She knew he would
avoid the board sidewalk and would scout the
town using back streets and alleyways.

The sun rose and the air heated. Inside the
house it was stifling. Billy drooped about the
parlor and only when Eli challenged him to
three games of checkers did the boy settle
down.

"I sure hope Uncle Hawk knows what he's
doin'," he confided as Eli jumped his king.

"He does," the gray-haired man replied.

"Your uncle's famous for knowin' ezactly what he's doin', so don't you worry none." He flashed Caroline a look from across the checkerboard.

"You neither, missy. Hawk'd die afore he'd let anyone hurt you."

That, Caroline thought with mounting anxiety, was what she was afraid of. She bolted from the faded wingback chair into the kitchen where Fernanda and Ilsa stood at the stove, ladling blackberry syrup into glass jelly jars. Fernanda took one look at her and folded the younger woman into her arms.

"I go early to pray," her companion whispered. "God is watch over you."

"And Hawk," Caroline murmured.

"*Si, mi corazón.* God will watch *Señor* Hawk, or I am speak hard words to the priest!"

Caroline tried to smile but found she couldn't control her mouth.

Ilsa turned to her and thrust an iron ladle into her hand. "Keep busy," she ordered.

"Is that why you are both making jelly in this ungodly heat?"

Both women stared at her as if she had just

announced the end of the world. "Yes, is why," Fernanda said, her voice quiet. Ilsa just looked at her, and Caroline read the censure in her gaze.

Don't hurt him.

She stepped forward and put her arms around Hawk's half sister. "I care for your brother, Ilsa. I am sorry."

Ilsa's eyes overflowed. "It's not your fault, honey. Hawk is too old to mind his big sister," she added with an unsteady laugh. "He is a man grown and stubborn, just like his pa."

She pressed the ladle Caroline held down into the simmering juice and took her place at the stove beside her.

Hours later twenty-seven pints of blackberry jelly sat cooling on the wooden counter, and Fernanda made both Caroline and Ilsa sit at the kitchen table while she made fresh coffee and sliced bread for chicken sandwiches.

Caroline discovered that she could take a bite of the sandwich, but she couldn't swallow. Ilsa pumped her a glass of water from the sink, but still she managed to choke down only half the sandwich. Billy gobbled the rest, and then Eli shooed them all out of the kitchen while he made a batch of sugar cookies.

Caroline paced from the front porch to the parlor and back to the porch. She saw Jericho Silver standing across the street from the house, his rifle barrel glinting ominously in the noonday sunlight. He saluted her with two fingers to his Stetson, and she tried to smile.

Where was Hawk? Was he watching people as they entered the meeting hall? Was he nearby?

A shudder snaked up her spine. Was *he* here, that man, whoever he was?" Oh, God, would she live through this day?

I have been waiting for this. Been watching you all these months and waiting for the right time. Been planning it carefully. I want it to be in public, when you are spreading your lies about men. I want you to be hurt.

Townspeople began drifting past the house in twos and threes on their way to the meeting hall. Women with placards marched by, their arms linked. Caroline imagined they were sisters, aunts, mothers, even grandmothers. Some were accompanied by men, none of whom looked pleased to be escorting their wives or sweethearts to hear a speech aimed at giving their women the vote and freeing them from the oppression of husbands and fathers and brothers.

She knew Hawk had convinced the newspapers to state that she was staying at the Smoke River Hotel; none of the passersby gave her a second look except for Verena Forester, who waved and smiled, pointing to the flounced green skirt she had sewed for her.

At half-past twelve, Hawk came to walk her over to the meeting hall. By then, Caroline had taken herself in hand and was feeling unnaturally calm. She slid one hand over the pistol hidden in her skirt pocket and with the other, took Hawk's arm.

Just as they reached the front screen door, Ilsa hurried forward from the kitchen, her blonde hair straggly from the heat, her gingham apron stained with dark berry juice. She took Caroline's hand in her own, and the two women looked at each other in silence. Then Ilsa nodded, leaned forward and kissed Caroline's cheek.

"Good luck," she whispered.

Tears clogged her throat, but she managed an answering nod and returned the pressure of Ilsa's strong, berry-stained hand.

Then she and Hawk stepped off the front porch and moved down the street toward the barbershop.

He carried no rifle she noted suddenly, just his revolver. A chill started at the back of her neck, but she ruthlessly quelled it and worked to force her spirit into a quiet place.

Fernanda followed them down the street with Eli, whose front pants pocket bulged with a weapon of some sort. Caroline knew Fernanda would be carrying her pistol.

Her footsteps slowed. All at once she didn't want to do this. Not now. Not with Hawk risking his life on her behalf.

"It's all right," he breathed beside her. "We're ready for him."

At his gentle tug, she moved on past Uncle Charlie's bakery and Verena's dress shop, past the mercantile where baskets of purple-blue plums glistened in the afternoon sun, to the barbershop and into the meeting hall behind it.

Inside, the heat was oppressive. She glanced longingly at the row of windows that ran down one side of the stuffy room, but Hawk caught her gaze and shook his head. Of course. He would allow none to be opened for fear of…

She closed her eyes and counted to ten. Behind her she heard the rustle of Fernanda's folded paper fan; how she wished she'd thought to bring one for herself. But she could not make a speech and fan herself at the same time, so perhaps it was just as well.

Hawk guided her down an uneven aisle forged in the middle of what looked like hundreds—no, thousands!—of chairs and benches of apple crates. At the far end stood a double stack of tall fruit crates, draped with what looked like an old bed quilt that served as a speaker's podium.

Hawk tipped his head at Fernanda, indicating a seat in the front row, next to his deputy, Sandy. Then he walked her to the podium, turned her to face the audience and laid his hand on her forearm.

"Give 'em hell, honey," he murmured. Then he stepped away and she looked out at the crowd.

Onlookers filled every seat and lined the walls and stood three-deep at the back of the hall. To her intense relief there were no children in the audience. In fact, no one under the age of fourteen had been allowed to enter. That was unfortunate in one way; young girls should grow into womanhood knowing their rights. In another way she was glad; if there was to be a confrontation, even—God forbid!—gunfire, she wanted no child to be accidentally hurt.

The guards she was used to seeing everywhere she went—Jericho and Sandy, Rooney Cloudman, and Colonel Halliday, and the Federal marshal Matt Johnson—were cleverly stationed around the room, blending in with the crowd lining the walls with their rifles hidden at their sides.

Oddly, there was no heckling. No catcalls. Just an ominous, heavy silence. Hawk must have arranged it this way. She knew none of the men in the crowd were asked to give up their guns; Hawk wanted to catch the man redhanded, and he feared that confiscating their weapons would tip him off.

Hawk lounged against the wall nearest her, barely the length of a bedsheet separating them. She locked eyes with him for a brief moment, then swallowed hard and drew in a breath.

"Good afternoon." She tried hard to smile at her placard-waving audience. A rustle of paper fans swept over the warm room as women sought to cool their overheated faces. Most of the men in attendance sat in uneasy silence.

"I know many of you may be feeling uncertain about the prospect of women gaining the right to vote."

She hesitated, then swallowed. "Let me assure you, gentlemen," she continued, "that it is not women who are your enemy. It is, instead, yourselves. I say this because you are alienating the goodwill, even the affection, of your wives, your sweethearts, your daughters and sisters, mothers and grandmothers by not allowing us to share in the decisions that affect our lives. And your lives, as well."

She paused and gazed out over the sea of upturned faces. Incredibly, no grumbles emanated from the men, and no protests erupted from the sidelines. In the back of her mind she wondered if *he* was hidden somewhere among them, and she shot a quick look at Hawk who—surprise, surprise!—stood nodding in agreement.

"Let me give you just one example," she went on. "All of you want schooling for your children, do you not?"

Nods and smiles greeted the statement.

"But do you realize that you mothers have absolutely no say about which teachers are hired and what subjects your child will learn?

These decisions are entirely in the hands of the school board, and that body comprises only you men! While I know you are all hardworking and capable parents, you are only one half of the partnership you entered into when you married and produced those children. Women have no vote on school board matters. In fact, in Oregon, a woman cannot even sit on a school board!"

This was greeted with surprised looks and murmurs of disapproval.

"Now, I ask you, is this fair? Is this the equality guaranteed by our Bill of Rights? Should only half of the citizens of Smoke River decide these important matters for your children?

Many in the crowd, both men and women, shook their heads, and Caroline felt a surge of hope. People were actually beginning to see the sense of empowering more than just fifty percent of the decision-makers.

"Women," she pressed on, "should not be the slaves of men. Your wives and daughters are not the possessions of you gentlemen, no matter how much they may be loved and valued. But you do not *own* them. They are free human beings, are they not? Therefore, do not women deserve a say in the matters that affect them?"

An undercurrent of agreement circled the hall and she pressed on. "Over a hundred years ago, we fought a war over the practice of taxation without representation. Is it not time for us to live up to what rights our forefathers won?"

She paused and took a sip of water from the glass at her elbow. "Now, I am sure you must have some questions."

An arm shot into the air. "'Scuse me, ma'am, but God made Adam first and then Eve. Don't that mean a man's more important than a woman?"

Caroline smiled at the man. "Do you honestly believe, sir, that your wife or your sister or your mother is less important than you yourself are?"

"Well…" He sneaked a guilty look at the gray-haired woman seated next to him. "Well, I guess not, when ya put it like that."

A bent farmer in overalls at the back of the room waved a gnarled hand at her. "What'll happen when women get the vote an' start runnin' things they way they want, huh? They'll want to upset ever'thin, sure as shootin'."

Male voices rumbled agreement. "Sir," Caroline interjected, "women constitute only half of your population. That is only fifty percent of the vote on any one issue. You gentlemen have the other fifty percent!"

A long silence descended. Caroline surveyed her audience and waited. She was making progress, she could feel it. She could almost hear their minds opening up.

"Are there any more questions?"

An older, heavily bearded man rose to ask a question. He wore a well-tailored pair of brown trousers and a loose-fitting fawn-colored wool jacket, and his wide-brimmed felt hat was tipped down at an angle that obscured his face.

"I've been following your speeches for some time, Miss MacFarlane. In Texas. In Arizona. And now here."

Caroline hesitated. The man's voice sounded familiar, but she couldn't place it. Or him. Had she seen him before?

"Do you have a question, sir?"

"You might say I've got a question, all right." He enunciated the words carefully as he moved into the aisle.

Hawk jerked to attention, his nerves quivering. Something about this man wasn't right.

Then the stranger slowly lifted his head, palmed his hat back, and smiled.

Caroline's face turned dead white. "Papa? *Papa?*"

"Thought I was dead, didn't you, Carrie? Well, I gotta tell you, little girl, I'm a lot tougher than you think. And besides that, you're a lousy shot."

Stunned, she stared at him. Why was he telling her this? Why was he here?

Then his right hand went to the pocket of his jacket, and Hawk was on his feet, moving toward her. Suddenly everything slowed down. It seemed to take hours to cross the few yards to where she stood frozen at the makeshift podium. Somewhere to his left he heard someone yell.

He saw the man's arm come up and aim a blued steel revolver straight at Caroline.

Her mouth opened in a scream and he lunged for her, knocked her to the floor and covered her body with his just as the gun went off. A scalding bolt of lightning bit into Hawk's back.

A roaring sound hit his ears and a flash of orange light streaked past his shoulder. He heard a man cry out and something heavy thumped onto the floor behind him.

A woman screamed. Someone shouted something, but it was cut off by the sound of chairs and benches overturning and people's footsteps scrambling for the exit. And a second gunshot.

He couldn't breathe, couldn't think. His vision went gray but he shook it off. *Stay conscious. Stay with it.*

Hands pulled at him but he clung to Caroline's shaking body beneath him.

"Let go of her, Hawk. The bastard's dead." Jericho Silver's voice.

He raised his head. Caroline's hand lay near his shoulder, her fingers clutching his shirt.

"It's all right, Hawk. She's safe." Sandy told him.

"How...?"

"She shot him. Must have had her pistol in her skirt pocket. Anyway, she fired just as you tackled her."

He tried to get to his feet, but a pair of strong hands held him down. "Lie still, you stubborn bangtail. You've got a bullet in your back."

That explained the heavy, burning pain between his shoulder blades. He could hear Caroline sobbing, feel her body move convulsively as he lay on top of her.

Out of the corner of his eye he saw two pairs of legs. One belonged to Elijah Holst; he recognized the worn jeans. The other had to be Rooney Cloudman, who still wore his faded blue army trousers.

"Gonna roll you offa her," Rooney said. "Gonna hurt some."

Some! It hurt like nothing he could ever remember, not even the knife slashes purposely

striped across his rib cage, courtesy of a renegade Mescalero out for revenge. He must have
started to bleed, because now his shirt felt wet
and hot.

Someone shoved a folded quilt under him.
It got sticky pretty fast, so he knew he was
losing blood.

Caroline scrambled to his side and bent over
him, still weeping. He opened his eyes, fighting to stay awake. Her skirt had a small black
hole in it. Hell, she'd fired right through the
pocket. He tried to smile.

Her small, warm hands lifted his head
into her lap and her tears kept dripping onto
his face. He opened his lips to tell her something… What was it? Seemed important, but
now everything was growing dark.

The last thing he heard was Caroline's bro-
ken voice crying his name.

Chapter Twenty-Six

He heard voices, one praying in Spanish and Caroline's, and then Ilsa's, then Caroline's again. His back and chest ached and he couldn't figure out where he was.

Footsteps pounded somewhere, light ones, like a kid wearing shoes too big for him. A door cracked open.

"Uncle Hawk?"

Billy. That must mean he was home, lying in his own bed. He wanted to open his eyes and see into the walnut tree outside his window, but his lids seemed to be glued shut. Head ached, too.

"Uncle—?"

"Shhhh," someone warned. "He is sleeping."

"He's been asleep for two days. When's he gonna wake up?"

The soft voice spoke. "When he is ready, *mi amiguito*. You tell your *madre, si?* Will be soon, I think. The *señor*, he make groan sounds."

The kid's footsteps receded, and then a breath of cool air wafted over him as someone else entered, someone in a long swishy skirt. Someone who smelled of roses.

"Go down and eat some supper, Fernanda. I will watch over him."

The door closed and Hawk tried again to open his eyes. He needed to see her, make sure she was unhurt. "Caroline." He rasped her name but could only utter that one word.

"Hawk," she whispered near his ear. "Don't try to talk. The doctor says you will be all right, but you must rest for a few—"

He caught her hand. "Tell me," he croaked.

She laid a cool cloth across his forehead but said nothing for a long minute. Then she released a long breath and he heard her settle onto his straight-back desk chair; it had always creaked when he straddled it, so he guessed he'd weakened the slats.

"You were shot, Hawk. It was my father who…" Her voice quavered. "Papa was aiming for me, but you—" She swallowed audibly.

"You dove on top of me and took the bullet instead. Oh, Hawk, I told you I had shot him ten years ago. I thought I had killed him then."

He squeezed her hand.

"Anyway," she resumed, her voice steadier. "Jericho and Marshal Johnson said that the bullet hit his chest, and this time I really did kill him. They said it was self-defense."

"Damn right," he groaned.

"I am not sorry that I did it. He would have killed me, and he almost did kill you."

"Not dead yet," he managed.

She lifted the cloth from his hot forehead and swung it over him. Whispers of cool air washed against his face. When she replaced it, it was cool again.

"Head hurts."

He heard her stand up, and her hand came to rest on his bare shoulder. "The doctor gave you more laudanum this morning. That's why your head aches. Try not to talk."

Someone came into the room and he heard faint whispering. Something about broth. His stomach rebelled at the prospect.

"No," he muttered.

"He has to eat something," his sister murmured.

"Maybe just some water for now, Ilsa."

Oh, God, yes. His tongue was so swollen with thirst it felt like a dusty saddle blanket.

The door opened and closed again and Caroline touched his closed mouth with something metallic. A spoon. "Water," she explained. She dribbled it past his lips, teaspoon by teaspoon.

"Then what?" he asked between swallows.

"Then they carried you up here to your room and the doctor…well, he cut the bullet out of your back. It was…pretty awful."

He had wondered what felt so tight around his chest; must be Doc had trussed him up like a Christmas ham. Or two. Felt like he couldn't draw a deep breath.

"Sorry you had to see it," he said.

"He tried to make me go downstairs, but, well, I wouldn't. I couldn't leave you."

But she would leave him, eventually. Wouldn't she? In a way he was glad he couldn't see her. There was something he wanted to tell her, but he could only squeeze out a few words, and that wasn't going to be enough.

"Caroline?"

"Yes, Hawk? What is it? Do you want something?"

He nodded, even though it made his temples pulse in agony.

"You. I…want you."

"Miss MacFarlane?"

The stocky man stepped up onto the front porch where Caroline sat with Ilsa and Fernanda.

"Rooney Cloudman, ma'am. Remember me?"

"Yes, I remember."

"How's he doin'?"

"Better," Ilsa said. "Doc says he'll be up and ornery very soon."

"Well, Miss MacFarlane, I'm sure sorry to

interrupt, but I had to bring you something. Found it in yer pa's pocket."

All the breath left her body. "What is it?"

Rooney studied the toes of his boots. "You looked so peaked after the funeral I thought about just losin' it by accident-like, but..."

He produced a folded sheet of yellowed paper. Caroline reached for it, and Rooney caught her hand and squeezed it. "You know, ma'am, you don't have ta read it iff'n you don't want."

She nodded and slowly unfolded the single page while Ilsa poured a glass of lemonade for him.

Carrie,
If you are reading this then I am dead or in jail somewhere.

I have wanted revenge for years, ever since you shot me and your mother took you away from me. I can't ever forgive that. Then she died and you stepped into her shoes and started speaking out, and that's when I knew what I had to do.

I had to stop you before you told about what I did to you.

Caroline sat for a long time with the unsigned letter in her lap. And then she tore it up in little pieces and put the bits of paper in her skirt pocket.

Chapter Twenty-Seven

Fernanda settled beside her on the cool front porch and lifted Caroline's hand into her own. "You must decide, *mi corazón.*

"I—I know."

"You care for this man, *si*?"

Caroline nodded, then buried her face in her hands. "Oh, Fernanda, I am so torn. I promised Mama I would carry on with her work. Well, it's my work, really. It is so very important, for all women, not just the ones out here in the West."

Fernanda looked at her in silence for a long moment. "In the country of my birth, this thing it is not important. But in Tejas, in America, such a thing it make a big difference. *Muy importante.*"

Billy clattered through the screen door. "Fernanda, you wanna play checkers with me? Eli's upstairs with Uncle Hawk, readin' some dull old book out loud."

The Mexican woman heaved herself to her feet and ruffled Billy's russet hair. "*Si*, I play checkers. If I win, you wash dishes, is true?"

Caroline had to laugh. Fernanda had made herself an important part of this household. "I will wash up the dishes," she announced.

Fernanda paused, her hand on the door frame. "No, you do not, *hija*. You have big decision to think about."

Hawk stood the inactivity of lying in bed for as long as he could, but after what he judged was three days, he got up and slowly and painfully pulled on his jeans and a shirt Ilsa had folded on the bureau next to the basin and pitcher of water. Then he walked unsteadily down the stairs in his bare feet.

It was almost supper time, he guessed. Fernanda was showing Billy how to set the table and Ilsa was at the stove, rolling out biscuit dough. Hawk sidled past them, noting his sister's accusing look and Fernanda's frown, and pushed through the back screen door. Sure enough, Caroline was in the yard, hanging laundry on the clothesline. Again.

All he could see behind the sheets swelling in the warm breeze were her shoes and the bottom ruffle of her white petticoat as it peeked out when she raised her arms.

He settled on the top porch step and waited. Getting down the stairs had cost him; he was breathing hard and his back felt like a bull had gored him.

She emerged finally, gave one sheet a tug to smooth it and started toward him. Damn she was one beautiful female. So beautiful it made his throat ache. She'd rolled the sleeves of her shirtwaist up to expose her elbows, and he had an insane urge to put his mouth on the flesh right there at the curve of her arm.

"Oh!" Her hand flew to her mouth when she saw him. "Hawk, whatever are you doing out of bed?"

"Got bored. Wanted to see you."

"My heavens, I would have brought up your supper on a tray later—"

"Don't want supper on a tray. Want it sitting down at a table. With you."

"Oh."

"How come you didn't come upstairs all day?"

"I—I've been busy, as you can see." She gestured to the flapping sheets behind her.

"You know, you hang up an awful lot of laundry for a speech-making lady."

"I did the washing, too. I…needed to keep busy. I needed to think."

"About what?"

"Hawk, you know about what. It's about, well, about making speeches."

"Yeah, I figured that. While you're doing all this thinking, I need to throw something else in the pot for you to consider."

"Oh? Wait, I see a wrinkle!" She escaped into the sea of muslin on the clothesline. With a groan, Hawk heaved himself off the step and followed. He caught her between two rows of drying pillowcases and blocked her escape.

"Hawk—"

He reached out and touched her bare arm. "There's something I want to tell you, Caroline. I've been wondering how to say it, but there's no easy way, so here it is. I want you to stay here, in Smoke River."

"You know I can't do that. I have a speaking engagement in Quincy next week, and—"

"Here in Smoke River," he repeated. "With me." He drew her into his arms and pressed his lips against her forehead.

"Hawk. Oh, Hawk, you have given me so much, protected me through all this mess and never once criticized me or what I had to say, even though I know you don't agree about the vote for women."

"Didn't once. Maybe I do now. You can be damn convincing."

"Really?" Her face lit up like a kid's on Christmas morning. "Do you mean it? Really?"

"Yeah. And there's something else I really mean, too." He held her gaze for a long minute. "I'm in love with you. Pretty deep, too."

"Hawk," she breathed. "You must know how I feel about you. You brought me back to myself. As a woman, I mean. Made me know that I could love someone. I am glad it was with you."

He guided her out of the forest of sheets and turned her toward the side fence. "See that house over there?" He tipped his head toward the white two-story structure next door.

"Yes, I see it. It's lovely, but—"

"It's empty except for a lot of furniture. Old couple, Monty and Ruth Monroe, used to own it until they went to live with their daughter in Montana. Left everything just as it was."

"It has a nice, big porch," she ventured. "A 'wraparound' they call it back East. But why…?"

"I want to live there."

"But you live here in this house, with Ilsa and Billy."

"I want to live there with you, Caroline. I want you to marry me."

Caroline stared up at him, then at the pretty white house, then back at Hawk. "You know I can't, Hawk. I might want to, but I can't. There is something I must do and I cannot give it up. It is my life's work."

"Figured you might feel that way. I wanted to change your mind."

She was quiet for a long time, feeling his arms around her as tears clogged her throat. The thought of leaving him was like a knife slicing into her heart. She raised her face and he bent to kiss her, slowly and thoroughly, leaving the taste of mint on her lips and her body aching in places she'd only recently come to appreciate.

She wound her arms around his neck and he flinched; she'd forgotten his bandages.

"Don't stop," he whispered. "I'd rather feel your mouth under mine than worry about miles of gauze around my chest."

She fought back an absurd need to weep and kissed him until they were both having difficulty breathing.

"Supper time!" Billy yelled through the back screen door.

"Oh, hell," Hawk muttered.

She laughed softly. "Hawk, you need to eat to regain your strength."

"I'll eat if you promise to think about what I said."

Her eyes filled. "I will. I promise."

But she knew what her answer would be, what her answer would always be. She had chosen her path years ago. She had promised her mother, and herself, and she must continue until the battle was won.

Fernanda studied Hawk, then Caroline across the supper table. Neither had spoken two words since they sat down. Billy chattered on about school starting in September and the big trout he'd caught yesterday. Eli reported on the doings at the *Sentinel* office and how mournful Noralee Ness over at the *Lark* office had acted ever since Hawk had been shot.

Ilsa dished up stew and biscuits and blackberry cobbler without a word.

What is the matter with my lady? And with Señor Hawk? They are both alive, thank our

Father in heaven. They are most foolish to throw strong feelings away.

She was glad when Billy pestered her for a game of checkers. Otherwise she would start to think black thoughts.

Is it only old women like myself who see life clearly? She shook her head. Such a waste, it was. *A man and a woman should be rich together.*

Harvey O'Grady stared at Hawk across the sheriff's paper-littered desk. "You gonna let her just walk away from you like that? Hell, Hawk, if I wanted her, I'd toss her over my shoulder and—"

"No, you wouldn't. That's rape, Harve."

The mayor blinked at him. "Rape? Well I'll be a—Hawk, she's got you so mixed up you're thinkin' like a tipsy leprechaun. You're startin' to sound like one of them damn women suffragettes."

Hawk looked at the mayor with dawning understanding. "You ever been married, Harve?"

"Well…yeah, I was married once. She up and left me."

"Ever ask yourself how come?"

"What? Whaddya mean? I ordered her not to visit the Widow Donohue and she did it anyway, and then she up and left. Damn near broke my heart. That woman *belonged* to me."

"A woman isn't something that 'belongs' to you, like a sack of wheat. A man doesn't just overpower a woman like a wild mustang or a cow."

Hawk topped up both their glasses, lifted his and downed it in one gulp. He couldn't feel any worse; might as well get jelly-legged drunk.

Chapter Twenty-Eight

Is very hard decision, to stay or go. I will miss Billy, *mi amiguito*. And *Señor* Hawk's sister, she work very too hard. I could be much help. But my lady, she does what she think her *madre* would want.

I know inside what *Señora* MacFarlane would want, and that is for her daughter Caroline to be happy in her life.

Why is this not simple? I ask the priest, but he have not an answer. I ask *Señora* Ilsa, and she weep and snuff her nose on her kerchief. Eli, he say women are foolish creatures, but Eli not so smart. He does not win me in checkers.

Me, I think it is mens who are foolish.
Even *Señor* Hawk does not think sharp
about this.

Dios, I do not know to do what.

Before dawn the next morning Hawk again
forced his aching body out of bed and into his
jeans and shirt. It wasn't going to be pretty,
but he had to settle some things.

The town looked deserted. The throngs of
visitors who had traveled to Smoke River to
hear Caroline's speech had departed for homes
as far away as Portland. Jingo confided over a
whiskey that he was making so much money
hauling passengers north to Gillette Springs
and beyond he was thinking about retiring to
raise goats.

He stepped through the door of the sheriff's
office to find Sandy slouched in the chair behind the desk, his hat over his face. The jail
was empty except for one sozzled cowhand,
sleeping it off in the back cell.

Quietly Hawk checked his messages, inspected the new Wanted posters, and read

over his logbook where both Jericho Silver and Marshal Johnson had made entries. Then he sat down heavily in the chair reserved for guests and acknowledged that he didn't have the stomach for law and order today. His head still pounded and he couldn't think clearly.

Caroline was leaving tomorrow morning.

Just how had it happened, this thing with Caroline? How had he been blindsided by a slim, starchy lady with a single mission in life—turning a man's life upside down?

Hell, she didn't need to get the vote to tip his life on end. All she had to do was stand there looking at him with those soft blue eyes and take the pins out of her hair.

Oh, hell, he couldn't let her leave.

He couldn't stop her.

Damnation. He felt like something was eating him alive from the inside out. Part of him wished that bullet had killed him outright. Watching Caroline climb onto that stagecoach tomorrow and roll out of his life would be a helluva lot worse than taking a bullet in the back.

* * *

At eight the following morning, Hawk walked Caroline out to the stagecoach waiting in front of the house. She gestured at the porch where Ilsa sat studiously avoiding her gaze while she shelled peas and Billy and Elijah bent over the checkerboard, wolfing down Eli's fresh batch of cookies.

"It is very hard to leave, Hawk. It is even harder to say goodbye to you." She turned to him and laid her hand against his cheek. "I will never forget you, Hawk. Never."

She knew this would not be easy, but she had no idea how much it would hurt. She felt like a wild horse was trapped inside her chest, stomping its way out with hooves sharp as razors. She bit her lip to stop its trembling. She could love a man and leave him to carry on with her own life, couldn't she?

Well, couldn't she?

"Hawk, please, kiss me now, before the others come to say goodbye." She stretched on tiptoe, felt him wrap his arms around her and lift her off her feet. He held her close for a long minute, then tipped his head to catch her mouth under his. His scent, of leather and wood smoke and mint, washed over her and her heart dropped into her belly and began to break into tiny, sharp pieces that hurt and hurt and hurt.

He lifted his lips from hers and set her on her feet. "You're more woman than I deserve, Caroline, but I want you anyway. I will always want you."

Blinded by tears, she turned to hug Billy and Eli and Ilsa one last time, then took a deep breath and pivoted toward the waiting stage-coach. She let Jingo hand her inside and set her canvas satchel at her feet.

"I'll get yer trunk when it comes in at the train station, Miss Caroline, and I'll send it on to Portland, like you said." He tipped his dusty hat to Fernanda and slammed the pas-senger door shut.

Caroline sat without moving, her eyes closed, her hands clenched in her lap. She couldn't bear to look out the window at Hawk, couldn't bear to see his drawn, tense face, and she did not want him to see her tears.

At last she heard the crack of Jingo's whip, and the horses jolted forward. She kept her eyes shut tight until the coach turned onto the town road, and then she stared straight ahead until Fernanda folded her into her arms and began to rock her like she would a child.

"Mi corazón," she murmured. "It will not hurt so much in time. But for now, you must bite down hard. *Hard.*"

An hour went by. Then another. Caroline stared out the stagecoach window, her mind numb. The landscape changed from rolling green hills to sagebrush-covered flatland and then to meadows with knee-deep golden grass and clusters of cottonwood trees where the road ran along the river.

She thought of Billy's pail of worms and about her tumbling headlong into the river when she leaned out over the water too far with her fishing line and baited hook.

Then her thoughts settled on the young girl in the pink pinafore, Manette Nicolet, who made Billy blush and stammer. Would the girl grow up to take part in the affairs of

Lake County? Vote as a member of the school board? Help elect a judge or even a senator? Oh, she did hope so.

In fact, she would write about this in her next speech, and she would do it right this minute. She withdrew a lined notepad and a stubby pencil from her pocket and began to write.

Wouldn't it be grand if every single speech she created could be sent—

With a cry she stopped midsentence and stared down at the paper on her lap.

Of course. *Of course.*

She leaned her head out the window. "Jingo!" she shouted, desperate to be heard over the noise of the coach and the hoofbeats of the team of horses. "Jingo, stop. *Stop!*"

Inside his office, Hawk heard the thunder of horses' hooves and the rumble of a stagecoach. That was odd. The southbound stage wasn't due to arrive until tomorrow morning, so what was—? He rose from his desk.

Jingo's shout brought him to the open doorway. The team slowed in front of the jail and before it halted the passenger door banged open and a slim figure in a flounced green skirt stumbled out and began to run.

"Hawk! *Hawk!*"

What the— He started toward her. "What's wrong? Did you forget something?"

She threw herself into his arms. "Hawk, I am such an idiot! I can carry on the suffrage campaign from right here in Smoke River. Oh, why did I not see this before?"

"See what before? Caroline, what are you talking about?"

She laughed and lifted her face to his. "Oh, don't you see? I can write—" She stopped to catch her breath. "I can write newspaper columns for every paper in every town and city in the country. From right here in Smoke River!"

Hawk heard the words pouring from her mouth but none of them made any sense.

And then suddenly they did.

"You mean you're not leaving?"

She nodded and started to cry. "I—I'm n-not leaving."

He stared at her flushed face and the tears

sheening her cheeks. "You mean you want to stay in Smoke River?"

"Yes."

"With me?"

"Yes!"

"You mean, uh, you'll marry me?"

"Oh, yes, Hawk. Yes!"

"Well, I'll be goddamned."

"Oh, yes," she said. "And I will be goddamned, too."

He gave her a swift, hard kiss. "Honey, what has campaigning for the vote done to your polite Bostonian language?"

"Oh, I don't care what it's done. All I care about is that it's brought us together."

Fernanda climbed out of the stagecoach and stood watching them, a sly smile playing about her lips. *My, my,* mi corazón. *You are not so stubborn like I had think yesterday. You make your* madre *very happy.*

The wedding took place the following afternoon in Ilsa's front parlor. Caroline wore a simple morning dress of yellow dimity and

Hawk dressed in the tailored dark suit he wore only on special occasions. Both were in for a gentle surprise.

Judge Jericho Silver stood at the fireplace, a Bible in his hands, as they recited their vows and Fernanda and Ilsa wept in the background.

"I, Anderson Luis Rivera, take this woman…"

"Anderson?" Caroline suddenly whispered. "Your first name is Anderson?"

"Yeah. My mother's maiden name," he murmured.

"I like it."

"She used to call me Sonny."

Jericho cleared his throat. "You two want to get married today or not?"

Caroline sobered. "Oh, yes. Let's see… I, Caroline Marguerite MacFarlane, take—"

Hawk blinked. "Marguerite?" he whispered.

"Yes. That was your mother's name, was it not?"

He nodded.

Again Judge Silver lowered his Bible. "Not sure we're going to get through this before midnight, folks."

Following the ceremony, Ilsa presided over a table loaded down with a four-tier wedding cake surrounded by yellow roses and Fernanda served gallons of coffee to half the population of Smoke River, which included Jingo Shanahan, and even Jonas Overby, who turned out to be an undercover detective.

The men kissed the bride, all except Billy, who stole a kiss from Manette Nicolet instead and blushed until his bedtime.

Halfway through the afternoon Fernanda took Hawk out to the front porch and sat him down in the swing. "*Señor* Hawk, I say something now."

Hawk looked up at her. "Yeah? I'm listening."

"Is about your *madre*. I know her for many years. Two things I say now. First is that your *madre* she go with your young wife to keep her safe, not to run away."

"Yeah, I figured something like that. Took me a few years, but I worked it out."

"Second is this, *señor*. Your *madre* would be proud that you protect Caroline. And most proud that you find love with her. *Comprende?*"

Hawk rose and gently kissed the Mexican woman on both cheeks. *"Comprende."*

That night Caroline and Hawk quietly moved into the house next door to Ilsa, which Hawk, just as quietly, had purchased from the Monroes. That morning he had sent Fernanda to put clean sheets on the big double bed upstairs.

And that is how I, Fernanda Elena Maria Sobrano, came to live in the town of Smoke River, in the Territory of the Oregon, named by the *Americanos*. God looks down and smiles on my lady and *Señor* Hawk. And me.

* * * * *

MILLS & BOON®

HISTORICAL

AWAKEN THE ROMANCE OF THE PAST

0816/04

MILLS & BOON®

The Regency Collection – Part 2

Join the London ton for a Regency
season in part 2 of our collection!

Order yours at **www.millsandboon.co.uk/regency2**

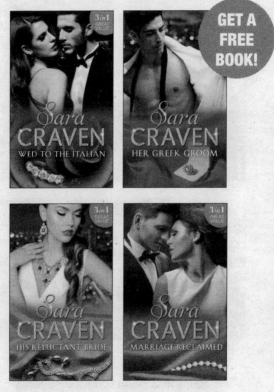